OMEGA'S DOCTOR

BABY MAKES THREE

BELLA BENNET

Illustrated by
COSMIC LETTERZ

CHAPTER 1

Ned wasn't sure why he was even here, wandering around trying to find someone that looked like they were waiting for a blind date to show up. Actually, he did know because Penny managed to guilt trip him into it. She could open her own law office and be as or more successful than her boss David. Ned shook his head. She could get you to agree without realizing what you had done. And by then it was too late.

So, here he was at 8:30 AM on a Saturday morning searching a public park looking for his blind date. He was the blind date for Penny's friend that was desperate. If this guy needed a date for a wedding why couldn't he find one on his own? What was wrong with him? According to Penny, the guy had gotten dumped and needed a date.

Oh well, Penny was right, he owed her for helping to bring their friends Henry and David together. And for loaning her cabin and doing the clean up. Probably more for the clean up. Ned shuddered. He was glad he didn't have to help clean up that cabin after a weekend of sweet, sweet loving.

Ned stopped and looked around again. There was a wedding party with relatives getting pictures taken in front of the park building. He had noticed no other party, so this must be the right one. He wished Penny had sent him the guy's Facebook profile or something so he could find the guy easier. Ned sighed and walked closer to the party.

As he approached, he realized that the party wasn't in the best of moods. The bride looked stuck up and kept sneaking glares at some guy. Hopefully that wasn't the groom. Nope, the quiet schmuck near her must be the groom. Poor guy. Oh well, he picked her so he had to put up with her.

"I don't know why he's doing this to ruin Melissa's wedding! Can't he grow up!"

"Shh, quiet. We don't want Fred's family to hear you. Act like nothing is wrong, then Steve won't get pleasure out of knowing how mad we are."

Steve? That was the name of the guy he was to meet. What was going on?

"I don't care! It is sacrilegious for him to bring a man for a date today! To his own sister's wedding! I can't believe he'd ever stoop this low. Where did we go wrong with him?"

"Be quiet. Just calm down. Steve said he had a man for a date but he's still by himself. He's bluffing just trying to make us all mad and be the center of attention again. Just ignore him."

Ned walked closer and glanced at the unhappy older couple. She looked like a piece of work. He'd recognize that judgmental, holier than thou attitude anywhere. Yuck. No wonder this guy Steve didn't want to endure this alone. He'd better find him and fast.

Ned continued walking towards the wedding party and skirted around the back of the crowd searching for Steve. He didn't want to call out his name or make it too apparent that he had no idea what the guy looked like. Ned didn't know what story Steve had told everyone, and right now after seeing his sister and parents in action, he was on board with playing this however Steve wanted. That sucked having parents like that.

Ned spied a guy standing apart from everyone trying to look like he was happy being there. That had to be Steve, but Ned wasn't sure. Because the guy was drop dead gorgeous. As in there was no way this guy couldn't get a date to a wedding. Which made him think the guy's personality had to be crap. Well with parents and a sister like that, what did he expect? Too bad he had to do a favor for the guy. But, he was here now, and it was too late to back out. If this was indeed his guy.

He walked closer and looked around. He still saw no one without a spouse or date. People were off in groups talking or wrangling the whiny kids. He didn't hate children, the kids here really were all whiny. The wedding photos with the children must have been going on for some time. Ned looked around again, but he had already checked out every male without an attached female over a certain age. None of them looked like they were looking or waiting for someone. The hot man had to be Steve.

Ned took a deep breath and focused on the smell of... nutmeg? He sniffed again and was sure it was nutmeg and another scent with it. Something that reminded him of Fall, apple cider and cozy nights in front of the fire. Mmm. He took another deep sniff and closed his eyes. Someone must be baking cookies. He opened his eyes and looked around. They were in the middle of a park. There was no bakery within the block. He turned around looking everywhere for the source of the smell. No one was carrying muffins or cider or anything. Then it hit him.

Ned swallowed, cleared his throat and walked forward. The guy heard the noise and turned around. And he thought the guy's profile was hot. Ned was tongue tied, and he wasn't even close to the guy.

The man smiled. "Ned, you made it!" He walked over and gave him a big hug. Ned hugged him back trying to will his cock to calm down and go back to sleep. That was hard to do when the hottest man besides a magazine cover model, was hugging you.

They pulled back and Ned could focus on the man's face. Black hair, blue eyes, chiseled jaw, high cheekbones and white teeth. Yup, a fucking gorgeous model. And he was a surgeon too? Whoever had dumped him was an idiot!

"Hi." Oh good job there, wow him with your eloquent prose.

"I'm so glad you made it. Did you find it ok? It's a little tricky with that quick exit and turn off the interstate."

Ned nodded his head. "Yeah."

Oh god, he was doing it again. Every time he was within the range of someone he had the hots for, he lost the ability to speak. How embarrassing.

"Good."

Steve wrapped an arm around his shoulder in a one armed hug and then walked them closer to the steps of the building. Ned calmed himself and was so focused that he forgot that he was a date and a distraction for Steve. Until something penetrated his foggy brain. Everyone was staring at them. No one came over to say hi. That was odd. Especially since Steve was related to the bride.

Ned leaned over to Steve. "Why is no one coming over?"

Steve put an arm around Ned's waist and leaned over. The heat from Steve's hand was burning through his suit jacket. "They're horrified I brought a man as a date. Sorry. But you were the only one that could make it on short notice."

Ned nodded. He didn't know what to do with his hands. Stick them in his suit pants or let his arms hang down like a monkey? He didn't want to show how nervous he was. Hands in the pockets it is.

"Do you need coffee? There's coffee inside for us if you need some." Here was a guy getting ignored by his own relatives and he was looking out for Ned's enjoyment. Ned's opinion of Steve changed, maybe he didn't have a horrible personality. But then again, five minutes of interaction wasn't enough time to form a full opinion.

"I'd love that. Thanks for letting me know." Steve winked at him and went up the stairs to the building. Ned paused, still in shock from the sight of Steve winking at him, and then followed him into the building.

* * *

STEVE HOPED he wasn't laying it on a little thick. He wondered if the arm around the waist or wink were too much. He didn't want to make his date uncomfortable, but he wanted it to look like they had known each other longer than five minutes. Which was the truth as they had just met each other.

And Ned was attractive. He had brown hair highlighted blond by being outside. Steve knew what salon highlights looked like, thanks to all the nurses he worked with trying to get his attention. Ned's were the real deal.

His natural scent had confirmed immediately that Ned was an alpha. A dominant woodsy, musk scent that reminded him of deep woods, camping and being protected.

Steve grabbed a styrofoam cup and got coffee for Ned. Then he stopped and turned.

"I'm sorry, Ned. I..I should have let you get your own coffee." He smiled so his embarrassment didn't show. He was treating Ned like a kid, who looked like he would be more than competent at whatever he did.

"No problem. It's nice not having to do everything." He smiled and winked back. The wink mesmerized Steve until he felt hot coffee on his hand. He jumped back and sucked his fingers. Damn, that hurt.

"Oh no, did I startle you? I'm sorry." Ned grabbed Steve's hand and wiped it off with napkins. Ned looked concerned and examined Steve's hand. Steve was more interested in examining Ned's face. He looked sun-kissed and fit. Steve wondered what he would look like without that suit on. Where did that thought come from? He should be focused on his sister's wedding not trying to score with his date of five minutes!

Steve looked back down at his hand, trying to ignore Ned. What was going on with him? "I think it's ok. Just a little hot coffee. It will feel better soon." Ned rubbed his thumb on

Steve's hand. That thumb movement worked for him. His cock was waking up and wanting to say hello to the nice man. He pulled his hand back and gave a smile.

"I'll get you another cup. I spilled this one." Steve tried to focus on moving the full cup over to the trash but he couldn't help but be aware of the body next to him. The fit, hot body next to him.

"Thanks. I'll get this one myself since I burnt you with the last one."

"Oh no, it was my fault." Steve looked up into Ned's eyes and knew he had made another mistake. Those brown eyes were smiling at him. No judgment, no conniving in them, no thinking of how he could use this to finagle more stuff out of him. It was refreshing not to have to deal with that. Which Steve didn't realize he had been dealing with, with his ex until now. Today was just full of personal revelations, wasn't it?

Ned drank out of his cup and swallowed. Steve couldn't help but watch Ned's throat as he swallowed. His skin was so smooth. Steve wanted to reach out and run his fingers down it and follow that up with his tongue. The clacking of heels pulled him out of his study of Ned's neck.

His mother was barreling down on them like a freight train. And she didn't look happy. Which was her usual expression for him.

"Steve! How could you! You're ruining your sister's big day by making a spectacle out of her wedding."

Steve clenched his jaw and looked over at Ned. Ned's eyebrows were stratospheric and he couldn't look anymore surprised if the Queen had shown up dancing the macarena.

"I want you to apologize to your sister right now and stop this charade. You're embarrassing the family!"

Steve flattened his lips and wondered how to get out of this without causing a scene, making his mother blow up even worse or giving in.

"I'm sorry but we haven't been introduced yet. I'm Ned Patterson."

Steve looked over at Ned and a happy warmth swirled through him. Here was a guy that didn't even know Steve, but was doing his best to draw the wrath of his mother away from him. He owed Ned big time.

His mother glared at Ned and said nothing. He had to do something and fast.

"Most mother's of the bride have a tough time at their daughter's wedding. I hope your day goes better." Ned moved his outstretched hand to wrap his arm around Steve. Now it was his turn to be surprised. "Why don't we go back and put cool water on your hand. Pardon us, ma'am." Ned guided Steve away from his mother and to the back hallway where the bathrooms were. Who was this guy? He was so smooth at handling his mother!

"You are amazing. I don't know how you could think let alone be so smooth. Thank you."

Ned smiled at him, with his arm still around Steve. "No problem. You were just caught in the moment. Something our parents can do to us no matter how old we are." Ned steered him into the bathroom and turned on the faucet.

"Get your hand under here. I think you should run cold water on it." Steve shook his head and laughed. He was the surgeon yet Ned, and he had no idea what his profession was, was the one doctoring him. It was nice to be taken care of. Thank God one of them was thinking.

"Again, thank you for your slick move at getting me away from my mother."

Ned winked. Steve looked down at his hand and wondered if that blush he felt was showing up on his skin. He hoped not.

CHAPTER 2

$\mathcal{N}$ed walked by Steve, back outside the building. The photos looked to be finished and better yet, Steve's mother was nowhere in sight. That woman was nasty. Ned couldn't blame Steve for not wanting to go through this alone. He couldn't imagine how hard it must have been for the guy, waiting to see if his blind date would show up or not. Ned reached over and put a hand on Steve's back. Steve jumped.

"I wanted to make you feel better. You know." Oh God, not again. Here he goes with the short sentences. And he thought he had gotten over that with the bathroom moment.

Steve flashed a quick smile and looked forward again. Ned dropped his hand. He felt awkward. Steve was Ned's idea of a walking wet dream. Nothing made him more uncomfortable than being next to a man he wished he could have.

Ned sneaked a peek at him. He looked like he didn't even do anything to look that good. Black hair not too short, appropriate business length as his old mentor would say. Those long black eyelashes were killer though. He bet woman would give their soul for eyelashes that long and thick. He smiled and looked back at the park.

The chairs were all set up, a fabric runner in the aisle between the chairs leading up to a veranda with a shelter. It was decorated with big ribbon bows and flowers.

"So, do we wait out here? Do you have a role in the wedding?"

Steve turned to Ned with a crooked smile. "Do you think they'd want me in the wedding?" Ned shrugged and felt bad for the guy.

"Why do they not like you so much, if you don't mind my asking?" Ned felt like a jerk for asking, but it was odd. Steve seemed like a normal, nice guy. Why would anyone shun that? Especially with him looking like a dream? Ned willed himself to look around at the chairs and stop drooling.

"No, it's ok. It's got to be hard for you to be with the odd one out at a wedding where you know no one." Ned shrugged, but he was right. It was odd.

"I don't know what the issue is to tell you the truth. Maybe my mother wanted a girl. Maybe I came too soon in the marriage. I have no idea."

Ned waited and then realized Steve was done talking. He looked over and narrowed his eyes.

"That's it?" Steve nodded his head. "You got no one pregnant in high school? Do drugs? Streak through the neighbor's graduation party?"

Steve raised an eyebrow. "That was pretty specific? Do I sense a story?"

Ned smirked and chuckled. "You did nothing crazy?"

Steve shook his head. "Not that I can think of. I don't understand it either. It's been like this my entire life."

Wow. That sucks. He had to be a head case growing up in a family that treated him like this.

"Well, I hope I can help you get through this crappy day."

Steve looked over and smiled. "You already have."

Ned stared and didn't want to look away. When Steve smiled, it was like seeing a perfect summer day, the fresh snowfall on Christmas morning or crossing the finish line first after a hard race. He was falling fast.

Ned gave a smile and looked away. What was he going to do? Should he get involved with a guy and be the rebound? He didn't want to be the rebound. Ned wanted to be the real thing.

He felt a finger brush against his hand and he glanced over at Steve. Steve wasn't looking at him. He was looking around at people moving to the pavilion. Maybe he didn't know he was doing it?

Ned looked at Steve who was watching people moving towards the chairs. Ned leaned over and took a sniff.

"What are you doing?" Steve had glanced back at Ned with a quizzical look.

Ned was embarrassed he had been caught. "I just wanted to confirm something. You smell nice." Oh that was smooth. He'd smack himself on the forehead if he was alone.

Steve chuckled. "And you thought it was me? Smelling nice?"

Ned sighed and realized he would not get out of this without sharing more. "It smelled like nutmeg and some other spice used in Fall cooking. You know like pumpkin bread, apple cider, stuff like that."

Ned decided that since he was already caught leaning over, he might as well get a good sniff in. He leaned over and took a big whiff of Steve's neck. He smelled so good, Ned almost licked him. Steve was definitely the source.

Ned leaned back and stared at Steve. He was dazed and turned on from the scent. He knew he was looking at Steve like he wanted to eat him and rub all over him. Which was correct. He wanted to do both things. But, he was at a wedding and needed to behave. So he looked away and focused on the people settling in the chairs. He supposed they should get a move on and sit.

Ned stilled and wondered if Steve's family would be so petty as to not have him sit with the family.

"Steve, we should go find our seats. Do you know where we're sitting?"

He had his hand on Steve's back and felt it when he stiffened. Looks like Steve wasn't feeling good about the seating arrangements either. He rubbed his hand on Steve's back, trying to calm him down and give him something to help him get through this. At least to let him know someone here cared.

"I'm not sure. I assume we're with the family. But, God knows. I don't even want to ask my mother."

"Is there a wedding planner or someone that would know?" Steve looked around and they both spotted the woman with a clipboard at the same moment.

"Let's go talk to her." Ned tried to keep his hand on Steve's back as they made their way over to the person who hopefully knew what was going on. Ned was just floored at how rude Steve's family was. There had to be more to it than Steve having done nothing. He'd think about that another time. Right now they had to get in their places.

* * *

STEVE WAS surprised at how much he liked having Ned's hand on his back. It felt like he was being taken care of that someone appreciated him. He felt warmth from that thought. It made him happy.

They reached the woman with the clipboard. Which was a little odd? Didn't ushers walk people to the right seating?

"Hello, I'm a brother of the bride. Do you know where we're to be seated?"

The woman flashed a surprised look and then looked down at her clipboard. She rolled her lips and looked up.

"It says you're in the third row, but there's only one seat reserved for you."

Steve stiffened. He had RSVP'd he was bringing a guest. Why did his sister change it? When were they ever going to stop screwing with him?

"That's a surprise. I replied to the invitation that I was bringing a guest. As you can see I have a guest with me. Are you sure there's not another chair reserved for a guest?"

She looked back down at her clipboard and then back up.

"You let Melissa's mother, which I suppose is also your mother, know you weren't bringing a guest last week. You can't go changing your mind like that."

Steve felt anger roll through him. Last week was when he got dumped. How did his mother know about that? And why would she assume he wouldn't bring a guest? He was infuriated because Ned was a nice guy and he didn't want to sit by himself surrounded by self-centered vultures.

"Well I don't know what to tell you. I never told my mother I wasn't bringing a guest. As you can see on your paper, it said two. Is there another seat available with the family for my guest? Otherwise we'll sit anywhere on the bride's side." Steve thought he stayed calm and yet still sound assertive. He was proud of himself. His mother's machinations had him throwing fits. Probably something she had been counting on.

The clipboard woman gave a small smile. "Sorry, we had to redo the plan when your mother said you weren't bringing a guest. She didn't want an empty chair in that row. You can sit anywhere past the reserved rows."

Steve flashed a small smile. He would not let this get to him. Even though he was ready to scream at his mother for being a bitch, again.

"No problem. Thanks for checking." Ned smiled at the woman and then put his hand on Steve's back and led him to the main aisle.

"I'm glad you aren't here alone. I can't believe how nasty they're being."

Steve felt warmth and contentment flow through him like a hot chocolate on a winter's day. It was amazing how calm he was being considering the crap he had already gone through and the wedding hadn't even started yet. He was glad Ned was here too.

Steve leaned over to Ned. "I am glad too."

He gave him a genuine smile and turned to go into a row on the bride's side. He recognized no one in the row already, but that was fine. As a matter of fact it was terrific. If he didn't have to sit with his relatives, it might make this ordeal passable.

He picked up the wedding program and read it even though he didn't care. It hurt every time he was excluded or kept out of family functions. He didn't have a part in his own sister's wedding. He was even sitting back among the crowd like he wasn't part of the family. It hurt every time, but he had to remind himself that it was on them. It was their problem.

He felt a hand on his thigh and looked down to see Ned's hand sitting on his right leg. Steve was surprised and a little worried what anyone would think. He looked around and realized no one was looking at them. Everyone was focused on their own wedding sheets or talking to people near them. He liked Ned's hand on his leg, it helped to ground him and keep him calm. A reminder he wasn't alone in the bullshit of the day.

Ned took his hand off Steve's leg. Steve caught himself from trying to keep Ned's hand there. But then he felt an arm around his shoulders and glanced over. Ned was looking at the wedding program and was otherwise ignoring Steve. He wondered if Ned was doing this to get back at his mother and sister. Was he pretending they were a couple per his request or was Ned was doing it because he wanted to?

The music started and everyone turned around to watch the bridesmaids walk up the aisle. The dresses were ugly lime green things with taffeta puffs on the shoulders. That was mean making bridesmaids buy a dress to wear once that was so hideous it should be burnt. Steve was thankful now he wasn't a groomsman. The lime green cummerbunds were atrocious. His sister must have picked them out. Did she realize they weren't in the 80's anymore?

The wedding march started, and he rose to stand with the crowd. His sister was smiling nodding her head like she was the Queen of England and the crowd were her subjects. His sister always had thought highly of herself but this was going too far. And was that a tiara on her head? He snorted and shook his head. Tiara's are fine with a veil, but not one that was taller than Ms. America's!

Ned turned back and rose an eyebrow at Steve with wide eyes. Steve mouthed 'I know' and they both grimaced. He was so glad Penny had sent Ned to be his date. He wouldn't have gotten through any of this without him. His eyes lingered on his profile and he thought again at how handsome Ned was. Why was he still single? He would snap that up in a heartbeat. He was nice, caring, concerned for others and fit. Very fit. Steve looked down but couldn't see his ass through the suit jacket. Too bad. Maybe he could get it off of him later. Steve stilled in shock at that thought. What was going on with him?

He turned forward and focused on pretending to be interested. Steve hated weddings, but had wanted to enjoy and be here for his sister, until her behavior this morning. Now he wanted to leave before they did anymore embarrassing things. He didn't want Ned to see how they treated him. Which was odd, considering he had only met Ned about an hour ago. And he was just Steve's pretend date. Why did he care what happened in Ned's view?

The rest of the wedding went on without a hitch. He tried not to laugh at the first reading though. Whose idea was it to make that poor girl read out of the bible without a podium? And to hold the microphone in one hand and keep the bible open with that wind? He shook his head. He bet it was his sister. She didn't care about the difficulties anyone else would have. He sure wished he wasn't like that himself.

CHAPTER 3

The wedding was over. It was the most boring part of any wedding day. Ned looked forward to the socializing and dancing but this one would be different. He had never gone to an early morning wedding, never been to one with no alcohol and no dancing. Ned did not understand what would happen during the brunch reception other than everyone leaving as soon as they ate. If there was no music or dancing why would anyone stay?

He smiled and clapped as the happy couple walked down the aisle. For weddings, it wasn't too long of a service. Now they could deal with the reception and leave. They shuffled out of the aisle and merged with the crowd to go to the park building. They didn't talk while they were in the big crowd. Ned just tried to keep Steve with him, but it was impossible without grabbing onto his sleeve. He gave up and just grabbed Steve's hand. He didn't want to ruin Steve's jacket by holding onto it, but he felt like a parent with a little kid. Which neither of them were. So hands it was.

It was nice holding someone's hand. He knew it was just to keep them from getting separated, but it had been awhile since he had held hands with someone. They kept holding hands even after they were out of the crush and everyone was spread out more. He didn't mind it though. Steve was a handsome man. Ned was getting a semi again wondering what Steve looked like under his suit. He wondered if there would be a way to spill wine on him... and then he remembered there was no alcohol at the wedding. He frowned. There's another reason you should always have alcohol at a wedding reception, so people could spill wine and use it as an excuse to get people out of their clothes. Come on! Ned shook his head at Steve's family again. What a bunch of angry prudes. They all needed to get laid.

Ned snorted to himself and looked over to see if Steve had noticed. He seemed in his own world. Didn't want to make him think Ned was some freak, walking around snorting like a hippopotamus or something. Do they even snort? Maybe a rhino. He liked the thought of a fierce rhino snorting better. He rolled his eyes at himself. Sometimes he was just too weird for words.

They walked up the steps to the pavilion building or what-ever it was called. The big park building where the brunch reception was held. If there was no alcohol, would there even be toasts? Could they ding the glasses for the newlyweds to kiss? How lame if they couldn't do that? Why even bother having anyone show up if there would not be any fun? He sure didn't want to be in their shoes. Starting a wedding off with no fun was not a good omen his book.

The front of the building had a cute seating chart on an easel. The tables were numbered, and you found your last name, and number to see where you were to go. That was better than just having the clipboard woman trying to get everyone to the right table. Score one for whoever came up with this idea. He bet it wasn't Steve's sister.

They were at a table near the back of the room. About as far from the head table as you could get. Oh well, that meant they would have a good time! The less they had to be around his crappy family, the better mood he'd be in. He felt for Steve. That guy had the shitty luck to be born to a family of cranky, judgmental prudes. Ned had found those that were the most verbal about religion were the meanest people he knew.

They let go of their hands to weave through the tables to their table. Ned noticed that it was right next to the coffee pots and hallway for the bathroom. This was perfect! He liked finding the bright things in every situation and he couldn't have planned this any better than if he had assigned the seats himself.

"This is a perfect location isn't it?" Steve looked at him like he had just spoken Russian. With a bad accent.

"We're as far away as possible and close to the coffee and bathroom. Perfect location!" He leaned back and put his napkin in his lap. Well, he thought it was an excellent location. Maybe Steve was upset over the location. He should get out of his head if that was the case. And Ned supposed that was his job, to keep Steve distracted. Well, he could think of a few ways to distract a hot man...

Ned grabbed the plate with the rolls from the center of the table and offered it to Steve. He smiled and picked one. Then Ned grabbed one, but it slipped and fell. Onto Steve's lap. Who hadn't put his napkin down yet? Oops. He better clean up that chocolate frosting on Steve's leg. Perilously close to his crotch. He didn't do it on purpose!

He grabbed his napkin and dabbed at Steve's lap and glanced up. Steve was getting a good blush going.

"I didn't do this on purpose, I swear!" He just ruined that by winking. But what can you do? You're rubbing at the lap of a hot man.

"It looks like my rubbing isn't getting it out." Oh my God. What did I say? Ned felt a blush starting but hoped he could fight it off. He kept one hand on Steve's leg as he dipped his napkin in water and went back to rubbing Steve's crotch.

He had a little smile on his face because he was fighting a huge smile. And laughing. This was insane. He couldn't have planned this better if he had tried. If he had tried the entire plate probably would have fallen on Steve's lap. And then there'd he'd be, bobbing for donuts off Steve's lap. Hoping to get the long john. Get it? He snickered and flattened his lips trying to stop. There was someone talking up front and he should be respectful. Not rubbing and causing a wet area on the front of Steve's pants.

Ned gave up, most of the chocolate icing was removed, but it looked like there were large wet spots on the front of his pants. Maybe he could hold a napkin in front of him the whole time? Ned leaned back in his chair and took a long swallow of his orange juice. He would not look at Steve. The guy was certainly glaring at him. Or frowning. He most probably wasn't looking at Ned with a 'come fuck me now boy' look in his eyes. That would be nice though. Maybe he could convince Steve that he needed to dry his pants in the bathroom. And he needed Ned's help.

Ned focused on eating his donut while somewhat paying attention to the front of the room. People were talking about how the two met. Boring. When could they get this brunch they were promised? If they had to sit through speeches first, he would die. Or eat all the donuts. It was a toss up.

Someone walked by him and he glanced up. Oh shit. It was Steve's mother. Ned turned to Steve. He had a pinched look on his face. Ned had better run interference. But how without making a scene?

"I see you found your new spot since you messed up the seating chart I had worked on. You always do everything in your power to ruin everything I hold dear."

Wow. She was a piece of work. He couldn't see Steve's face but knew he had to be biting his tongue. Ned put his arm around Steve's shoulders to let him know he wasn't alone. And to piss off Steve's mother. That was the main reason he did it if he was being honest. Which he liked to be.

Her eyes moved from Steve to him. He smiled and waved with his free hand.

* * *

STEVE SAW his mother's eyes widen and then squint. That along with her pissed as hell look made Steve glad he was in public and his mother couldn't say anything with all these people around. She could be very nasty when she wanted to be. Which was almost all the time with him. He still didn't know why, but he gave up trying to figure it out a few years ago. Now he waited for his mother's reaction to whatever Ned had done behind him.

She looked to Steve again. He sat back due to the look in her eyes. Maybe he wasn't her son? He didn't think mothers looked at their children like they would actually kill them.

"You are despicable. You're ruining your sister's wedding by making a spectacle of it! You have no shame!"

Steve was stunned she would be so nasty right now. He was sure she wouldn't do anything so bad with witnesses, with people in the room they had liked and wanted to impress. He was so shocked that his mouth was open and he couldn't think of anything to say.

"Pardon me, but I can't help but overhear this, as the entire rest of the table."

Ned was speaking up from behind him. Steve wanted no one to fight his battles for him, but he didn't know what to say other than 'get the hell out of my face'. Which was not a good idea when you're trying to be quiet at a wedding reception.

"Do you think maybe you could table this until the reception is over? You don't want to take the spotlight off your daughter, do you?"

Steve bit the inside of his cheek wondering how bad his mother would blow up. She hated to be told what to do, especially that she needed to change her behavior. He was worried she'd throw things, or cry and wail at the top of her lungs. Steve felt Ned put his other hand on his leg and he was glad for the touch. He wasn't alone, and she would not treat him like crap with Ned here. Steve felt like smiling.

His mother pursed her lips and flared her nostrils. She looked ugly. Nasty ugly with her face pinched like that. She looked like that psycho teacher in those Harry Potter movies.

Steve's mother looked around at the table. Steve looked too. Everyone at their table, and the tables next to them were watching. Oh boy, this would either make his mother go for the big scene to get sympathy or to slink away and go even bigger when she got him alone. He hoped she slunk away. Please, let her go away.

He turned back to his mother just as she whispered 'This isn't over' and walked back to the front. He let out a huge sigh of relief. Thank God she didn't go for the big blowup. Most probably because Ned was here. He owed Ned a huge thank you.

"I'm sorry that had to happen. I hope I wasn't the cause of it. I thought nothing of it putting my arm around the back of your chair."

Ned pulled his arm away but Steve turned in his chair and put his arm on Ned's shoulder. "Don't. Please. You did nothing wrong. It was my being here, or my screwing up her seating chart, or it's a day that ends in 'Y' that caused her to be upset. You did nothing wrong."

Ned smiled and put his arm back. Steve leaned in closer. "I don't know how I would have gotten through this morning so far without you. Thank you so much."

Ned squeezed his thigh and turned back to the front. Steve grabbed his napkin off the table and put it over his lap. He couldn't believe he was getting a semi from Ned squeezing his thigh. Probably just an emotional reaction to having someone stand up for him. That was probably it.

Having figured out why his body was reacting to a man, he tried to focus on the head table, and not the arm around his shoulders, or the hand on his thigh. Which was hard. Considering he was semi hard himself.

His stomach rumbled thinking of food. He hoped they would get this show on the road so they could all eat. Why hold everyone hostage until his sister was done talking? She had been up there talking for a while now. Even before his mother stopped by.

Steve shook his head and took a drink of his coffee. He damn near spilled coffee all over himself when Ned moved his hand on Steve's thigh. He hoped no one else had noticed that jump. Steve glanced around but since they were at the chairs closest to the back of the room, no one else had seen it. He glanced at Ned wondering what the hell was going on, but he was focused on the front table. It looked like he might not even be aware he was doing it.

Steve didn't want to call attention to it by asking Ned to stop. He wanted no one else at the table to know what was going on. So Steve tried to ignore it. He took another drink and put his cup down. Thank God he did because Ned now was moving his pinky around. Which was moving near the inside of his thigh. His semi was getting more than a semi now. Dear God, had he been that hard up to get aroused from a man rubbing the inside of his leg? Steve swallowed and tried to pay attention to his sister. That should cure a semi.

CHAPTER 4

*N*ed figured he was going to hell. That had to be the only destination for someone that was trying to tease a man during his sister's wedding. Even though he was doing it to provide a good distraction for the man in question. He still couldn't believe how nasty Steve's mother was. Ned would never have believed it if he hadn't witnessed it with his own eyes.

He kept rubbing Steve's thigh up and down and running his pinky over the inside of his thigh. Ned didn't know what Steve did to keep in shape but that thigh was rock solid. He'd have to ask him if they could ever talk again. Ned heard Steve's stomach rumbling. He was hungry too. And not for food.

Ned sighed and tried to find something else to focus on besides the hot man beside him. The bride, Steve's sister had finally sat down. Oh good, now we can eat. Nope, the groom stands up. My God, do they not realize that no one can eat until the head table goes to get food? Who decided that we all needed to be held captive?

Ned looked over at Steve to see how he was taking it and found those bright blue eyes looking back at him. With desire. Lots of desire. Ned kept staring at Steve, rubbing his thigh and running his pinky as close to Steve's crotch as he dared. It was amazing how good looking Steve was. Again Ned was surprised that no one had snapped Steve up. Ned would have grabbed him with both hands and ran with him if he had known there was someone so amazing that was available.

Ned moved his hand off Steve's thigh and took a drink of his coffee. He jumped when he missed his mouth. Then he saw that his jump had caused more coffee to spill out of the cup, right onto Steve's pants. Oh shit. Steve would think he was the clumsiest alpha ever.

"I'm so sorry! I can't believe I did that twice. Please, forgive me, I just... I'm not normally this careless." How could he explain that it was Steve himself that was so distracting?

Steve stared down at his pants, like he couldn't believe what he was seeing. There was a huge coffee spill on the right leg. No hiding that sucker.

"We should go in the bathroom and wash it out. I'm so sorry." Ned turned to the table. "Excuse us, I made a mess again. I spilled the coffee all over his pants. It will stain if it doesn't come out right away."

Ned stood up and pulled Steve up with him. He made a show of trying to rub the coffee out, just so everyone could see the reason for their leaving the table. He didn't want Steve to get in trouble for randomly leaving the reception. Then he pulled Steve in front of him and led him to the bathroom in the hallway.

Steve pushed the door open and after Ned went through, he turned around and locked it. Steve looked surprised when Ned turned around.

"We want no one coming in while your pants are off." Steve's eyebrows shot up and he backed up.

"The coffee? On your pants? Take them off, I'll scrub it out."

That seemed to have gotten through to Steve and he unbuckled his belt, pulled down his pants and handed them over to Ned. Nice legs and very nice boxer briefs. Ned had to swallow and try not to make it obvious that he was staring. Well, he had work to do.

Under the cool water, or was it hot water? Ned couldn't remember. Might as well try hot then. He noticed a blow hand dryer in the bathroom. They could hold the pants up to that and get them dry. He wondered if they could devise some way to keep the pants up there but let them do other things without having to hold up the pants. Ned wondered if Steve would be up for some distraction since they were in the bathroom and seemed to have it all to themselves. If he would do anything, it had to be quick before anyone needed to get in.

Well it was a disaster. He got the coffee, as far as he could tell, out of the suit pants, but the water went through the front of the pant leg, to the back of the pant leg. The entire pant leg section was sopping wet. He looked up at Steve and grimaced. He didn't think oops would cut it.

"Uh, I'm sorry. I didn't think it through. Maybe there's a hair dryer in the women's bathroom we could use. Or wherever they were getting ready. Did they use a separate room to get ready instead of the women's bathroom?"

Steve had closed his eyes and ran a hand down his face. Now he was looking at Steve with his hand over his mouth. His eyes didn't look thrilled.

"Well, I'll check." He wouldn't stay here when he was in trouble.

Ned opened the door and realized they had a new problem. How was Steve going to cross the hallway, that everyone could see, with no pants on to get to the other room with the hair dryers? Ned walked across the hallway and opened doors. Maybe he could bring the hair dryer back to the men's bathroom. If there was an outlet in there. Wouldn't there be an outlet?

Ned opened a cleaning supply closet, a coat closet and then hit the jackpot with a nursing room or something. Makeup, clothes, hair dryers, curling irons scattered all over the counter in front of a big mirror. Ned wondered if they could lock the door and get busy. He was sure Steve wouldn't be up for it. Dammit.

Ned grabbed a hair dryer and went back to the men's bathroom. Steve was still there. He looked around but didn't see an outlet. Ned wanted to put his head in his hands, but he was holding wet pants and a hair dryer. He had no hand free to smack his forehead.

"I need to go back to the dressing room to plug in the hair dryer. With everyone looking up at the head table, I bet you could run across and no one would notice."

"Are you kidding? Whoever is up there talking would see me!"

"Well, if it's your mother, you could always moon her." Ned shrugged his shoulders. "It's a once in a lifetime opportunity!"

Steve just looked at him like he had come from Mars. Steve needed to lighten up and live a little. Ned probably wouldn't do it either, but with that kind of mother, he would consider it.

Steve went out of the bathroom and across the hall back to the dressing room. He plugged in the hair dryer and dried Steve's pants. The door opened and Ned looked up to the mirror to see Steve slipping inside. Ned was shocked. He didn't think Steve had it in him.

Now that Steve was here, Ned lost his nerve with his seduction thoughts. He sighed. That's why he had never tried it before.

* * *

STEVE'S HEART was still beating fast from just walking across the hallway. He figured it would be less noticeable if he walked a normal speed instead of running like he wanted to. Talk about having nerves of steel. Thank God he was used to controlling his emotions and keeping himself calm as a surgeon or he wouldn't have been able to make it across the hallway.

This had to be the craziest or most asinine thing he's been part of since his college years. Drying his pants in the dressing room during his sister's wedding reception brunch thing? Definitely a top ten in his life.

"Do you think this will work?"

Ned turned to look at him. "Well, we've got nothing else to try so I hope so."

He turned back to the pants and then glanced back. "I'm sorry this is turning into a disaster. I didn't mean for your pants to get so soaked that we had to dry them with a hair dryer!"

Steve gave him a quick smile and then jumped on the one thing that stood out in that declaration.

"So you planned on the pants getting soaked?"

Ned glanced back in surprise. "No! Of course not. I certainly didn't plan it. I'm just saying... I didn't mean for my washing them out to get them so soaked." Ned looked back to the hair dryer and wet pants.

"You have to admit, you did manage to get me out of my pants pretty fast." Steve leaned back against the counter and crossed his arms. He would make Ned squirm.

A light blush was on Ned's cheeks which made Steve smile. It was so obvious that Ned was interested in him. With the rubbing of his thigh and the pinky brushing his crotch, it was all Steve could do to not get a boner during his sister's wedding reception. Ned would pay for that. Right now.

Steve stood up from leaning on the counter and walked over to Ned, who was still busy staring at his wet pants. He believed Ned when he said he didn't mean for the pants to get soaked. They were soaked too. It would probably need a dryer to get dry, not a hand held hair dryer.

He stood near Ned and put his hand on Ned's back while he leaned over to look at the pants. "They still look... wet."

Steve had to bite his lip to keep from laughing. This blatant seduction was so out of character and over the top for him that he wanted to bust out laughing. He sounded like a bad porno.

He ran his hand down Ned's back and had to keep from smiling when he saw Ned get nervous the closer Steve's hand got to his ass. And from the short glimpses he had of it earlier, it was a mighty fine ass. He ran his hand over that ass now and squeezed.

Ned turned to face Steve. The hair dryer wasn't even aiming at his wet pants on the counter anymore.

"Be careful where you point that thing. It's... hot." Oh my God. He would smack himself. That had to be the worst line anyone has ever used. Especially regarding a hair dryer.

Ned looked flustered and unsure of what to do. Steve bit the inside of his cheek to keep from smiling but it was very hard to keep himself under control. He wondered if Ned had never been surprised like this before.

"Why don't you set the hair dryer down and point it at the pants. That way you won't have to hold it." Steve grabbed it out of Ned's hand and positioned it on the counter to blow at the big wet area on Steve's pants. Those poor pants. They would be so wrinkled after this.

"I feel at a disadvantage here, without my pants on. I think you should be fair and take off yours." Steve reached down to unbuckle Ned's belt. He had never been so bold in his life. It was if he was playing a part and went all in. He should get an Oscar for sure for this performance.

Ned reached down and tried to swat Steve's hands away. "Anyone could come in!"

Steve smiled. Ned looked worried. "Well then, we need to make it fast." He didn't know what would happen after he got Ned's pants off. He was making this up as he went.

The belt was undone, Steve was pulling the zipper down and then let the pants drop. He couldn't see anything due to Ned's shirt in the way. He wasn't sure what all they should do in here, anyway. The odds were high they would get interrupted.

"Now we're on the same level playing field." Steve looked down again and noticed Ned's socks. He busted out laughing. Ned had on bright blue monkey socks!

Ned smiled and stepped out of his pants. "Do you like them?" He struck a pose. "They're Happy Socks! I love their crazy socks."

Steve so far loved everything about Ned, and these socks just confirmed that Ned was a fun guy.

"I love them. They match your personality. Fun loving." They both smiled at each other. Steve wasn't sure what to do next, his seduction plan had deserted him.

"Now we're both without our pants, what should we do? Can you think of any way we could pass the time?" Ned walked up to him and ran his hand through Steve's hair. That felt so nice that Steve closed his eyes. He loved getting his hair washed by others. Getting a head massage was close to orgasmic.

"I love how bright your blue eyes are against your light skin. That combined with your black hair is just delicious. You're so beautiful."

Steve opened his eyes to see Ned right in front of him, staring at his face, running his hand over his cheek, jawline, back up the other cheek. He then pulled Steve's head forward and their lips met.

Tentative soft kisses at first. Like they were both wild animals scared of spooking the other one. Steve put his hand on Ned's hip. They were almost the same height but Steve was just a bit taller.

Warmth rolled through him at the feeling of being wanted and appreciated. He wanted Ned from the first moment he saw him. Their kisses were more forceful now. He was very interested in getting to know Ned better. His dick was trying to jump out and make an introduction all his own too.

He turned his head to get a better angle to kiss Ned, pull at his lips, slide his tongue in Ned's mouth. His desire was building. He put his other hand on Ned's ass and squeezed. Such a firm, tight ass. His bicycling sure paid off. He couldn't wait to see Ned's abs. The man had to be stunning with no clothes on.

His desire was building and building. Steve wanted to run his hands all over Ned, to take off that jacket and shirt and feel the muscles of his back, to lick his neck, to see if the firm ass matched his imagination. He let his desire come through his tongue and lips. He was driving himself into a frenzy. That semi he had been sporting was more than a semi now.

He pulled himself closer and wasn't ashamed to straddle Ned's thigh and rub his cock against Ned's leg. Ned was such a good kisser. He pulled on Steve's lower lip, dragging it out as he looked in Steve's eyes. The desire, want, need, hunger called to Steve. He moaned with want and longing. Steve's fingers dug into Ned's ass and hip. He pushed harder against Ned's thigh.

Steve pulled back. There were several inches between them. The cool air was a shock against his legs and hot cock. He whimpered from the loss of contact. Steve was satisfied to note the dazed and hungry look in Ned's eyes. Ned wasn't unaffected.

"We've got to get back. I bet it's been over 15 minutes already. As much as I want to find out how good the rest of you feels, it would be a bad day for someone to walk in on us."

Ned was the voice of reason. Steve felt like saying no and throwing caution to the wind. He wanted Ned. The strength it took to agree with him and not pull him back and begin dry humping his leg, was harder than anything he had experienced before. No one had turned him on so fast. It was like Ned knew his body.

He nodded and turned around. If he had to go back out there, he didn't want to do it with massive chubby. He ran his hands through his hair, patted it down and looked in the mirror to make sure he looked respectable. There, he was calming down. He had to remind himself that he was at a wedding, his sister's wedding. Just an hour or less and he could leave. He was sure he could convince Ned to spend more time with him.

Steve looked over and his pants were still damp. He wasn't sure they had gotten dried much at all. He would not glance at Ned. It would weaken what self control he had over his body. Steve grabbed the pants and put them on. The spot was too far down to be hidden by his suit jacket, but at least it wasn't high enough to make it look like he pissed himself. Or worse, came in his pants.

Ned shut the hair dryer off. He had pulled up and buckled his pants already. Steve glanced at the door.

"Do you think they're done giving speeches yet? Before the food?" He still couldn't believe his mother and sister. Go figure they'd make the wedding as intolerable as possible for everyone.

"I guess we'll find out. I hope we got your pants at least a little dry."

Steve chanced a look at Ned. "Oh, I think we heated them up." With a wink he turned and opened the door to the hallway.

CHAPTER 5

$\mathcal{N}$ed followed Steve to the buffet. He was moving on autopilot as his brain was still back in the dressing room. His brain was stuck on that kiss. Or that series of kisses. He was blown away by Steve's skill in making just a kiss be so much more. He felt all the attraction, want, desire in Steve's lips and tongue.

Ned reached up to touch his lips. They were still tingling from their kisses. He couldn't remember the last time, if ever, he had almost cum from kissing. Not even when he was a randy teen and was horny all the time. That man knew how to kiss. He wondered what else he could do so well. No, stop thinking about it! He had just gotten himself under control.

Everyone was getting in line or moving back to their table and hadn't noticed their coming back. Ned felt awful that Steve's pants were still damp, but at least they had an excuse for coming back after so long, if anyone asked. He was sure Steve's sister and mother would have something 'pleasant' to say about that later. Ned couldn't believe how nasty Steve's family was. If he were in Steve's shoes, he wouldn't have bothered showing up. Steve was a better man than he was.

They reached the buffet, and he piled his plate with whatever low carb food he could find. He was surprised that the buffet looked good and not full of toast, pizza and Mountain Dew considering how trashy Steve's sister was. They made their way back to the table and dug in. He didn't know about Steve, but he didn't want to spend anymore time here than he had to. Plus, he felt protective of Steve. No one should have to deal with bullshit like that from their own mother. He would get Steve out of here before his mother made another appearance.

Ned glanced over at Steve and he seemed to be hell bent on eating as fast as possible. Ned smiled and turned back to his food. They were not staying for the cake cutting or anything like that. Were they even going to have a cake cutting? Ned took a drink of his coffee while looking around. Nope, he could not spot a cake. What an odd wedding this was.

He went back to eating and ignoring the people at the table. They must not be relatives as no one tried to speak with them. He also doubted that Steve would have been sat with relatives considering how his sister was. That was terrific for Steve's sake. He may just be a blind date, but he felt for Steve. And he felt an intense attraction to Steve as well.

He drank several gulps of his coffee and then looked around. Steve's mother was still at the head table. Yes his parents had sat themselves at the head table. Ned shook his head. He looked and made sure Steve's sister was still up there. Then he leaned over to Steve.

"Are you about done? Your mother and sister are at the head table still. We could probably sneak out the back door if you want to leave without them getting ahold of you again."

He put a hand on Steve's thigh to balance himself and to keep himself from kissing Steve. That urge was so strong it was almost like a compulsion had taken him over. As far as he knew there wasn't a full moon. He had never heard of the full moon affecting sexual urges, but he knew the ER at the hospital he worked at would always be extra busy around the full moon.

"Thanks for looking out for me. Yes, I would love to get out before they figure out we've gone. My car isn't too far from the building. What about yours?"

"I parked farther away. I wasn't sure where to go so I'm at the other lot, the farthest one from the building but closest to the pavilion where they got married." Steve nodded his head.

"We'll go to my car and come back later for yours. That sound ok?" Ned couldn't hold back a smile.

"That meshes with my plan." He stared at Steve, the hunger and desire in his eyes matching that of Steve's.

"Why don't you get up first. I'll follow a few minutes later. I can run to your car if I need to." He was hoping it wouldn't come to that, but with how crazy Steve's mother had already been today, he didn't know how much crazier it would get.

Steve leaned over and gave him a quick kiss on the cheek and then stood up. "I'm hitting the bathroom, I'll be right back."

Ned nodded his head and sat forward again. He looked around and wasn't surprised to see that so many had already left. Ned was surprised they had enough to fill the room at the beginning. He didn't think people with personalities like that would have many friends.

Ned looked down at his watch and decided that enough time had passed. He put his napkin on the table and left. He walked down the hallway and out the back door. Ned stopped himself from looking back and continued to walk to the parking lot to the left of the building. He saw Steve standing by the car. Ned smiled. Steve was a great guy. He was amazed again that he had no one to go with him to this wedding. But then again, Ned was enjoying this so he wouldn't complain.

Ned opened the door and got into Steve's car. "I'm amazed we pulled that off. I thought we'd be stopped at the door or someone would get on the microphone and tell everyone to tackle us."

Steve laughed. "The thought crossed my mind. I would not have put it out of the realm of possibilities for my mother. She is bat shit crazy."

"You are not kidding. I couldn't believe how nasty she was to you before the reception started. And in front of all the people at the table!" He shook his head, thankful yet again that he had no one crazy like that in his family tree.

Steve pulled out onto the main street and picked up speed. Ned relaxed and breathed easier. He didn't realize how worried he had been until they got away scot free. "I don't know about you, but I am relaxing now we are on our way out of there."

"Yeah, I didn't realize how nervous I was until I started the car and backed out. I could collapse from the stress alone."

Ned put his hand on Steve's shoulder and squeezed. The poor guy. Think of having to grow up in a house with that woman. Yuck.

"So, where should we go? Play pool? Watch whatever game is on? Go back to your hotel?" Ned thought he'd put that out there and see what Steve thought. He hoped he wasn't too forward, but after those kisses in the dressing room, well he was sure ready for more and to find out what else Steve could do with that nimble tongue.

Steve looked over and smiled. "You read my mind. My place it is."

* * *

STEVE LED Ned to the room he had booked at the hotel. He could have gone to his apartment, but he hadn't been sure if any relatives would follow him and tell his mother where he lived. He had to keep his home a secret so she wouldn't show up out of the blue. Like she'd done before, many times. She was not conducive to a stress free life.

Steve opened the door but let Ned walk in first. It was a plain room, nothing too fancy. But it had a bed, which was the most important and only thing on his mind. He wished he had sprung for a hot tub on a deck or in the room. But those rooms were way too expensive, plus he didn't know he'd be bringing someone back with him. He'd have to thank Penny for sending Ned. He was a perfect date, kept him distracted today.

Ned loosened his tied and turned around. "I could use a drink or two after that. Crazy makes me thirsty."

Steve laughed and nodded. "Yeah, I always work up a thirst trying to avoid them. It's stressful being around them even if they ignore you. I don't know what's in the fridge but we could always go down to the bar."

Ned removed his tie and jacket and opened the room fridge. He cringed and closed the door. "I think we will need room service unless you like Bud."

Steve grimaced and shook his head. "No thanks! Room service it is."

Steve called down for some liquid refreshment while Ned went in the bathroom. He had no condoms with him as he hadn't planned on getting lucky at his sister's wedding reception. That was too Alabama for him. Which was a horrible stereotype, he was sure some people from there didn't date at family gatherings.

Drink order placed, Steve took his jacket and tie off. He didn't know how to bring up the subject of condoms. He hadn't picked up someone and brought them back after just a few hours for a long time. What was protocol here? He didn't want to get in the heat of the moment and have it fizzle out because no one had protection. But then again, he didn't want to drive to a pharmacy and then come back. This dating thing was hard.

Ned came out of the bathroom unbuttoning his shirt. Steve stared and was well distracted watching Ned unbutton several buttons. Then Steve shook himself. It was times like these that he hated the self control he had.

"Before we go any further, I want to tell you I haven't got any condoms. I wasn't prepared to pick up anyone at my sister's wedding."

Ned smiled and pulled off his shirt. He had a well muscled nice chest. Well muscled and tan. Steve licked his lips as his mouth got parched. He wanted to run his tongue over those pecs, down his abs and follow the happy trail to Ned's pants. What would he taste like? Those arms were divine and muscled too. Whatever Ned did besides bicycling, it was sure working for him.

He looked back up at Ned to find him smiling at Steve. Ned approved of Steve if the monster trying to poke out of his pants was any sign.

"Don't worry about the condoms. I threw some in my wallet this morning, just in case. Penny's friends seem to be fantastic looking people. I was hoping I'd be able to use them today, and I was right. You are incredibly handsome."

Steve smiled and reached out to run his hands over Ned's shoulders. The heat of Ned's skin was arousing. Hot skin on a hot body. Steve took his time running his hands down Ned's chest, feeling the muscle definition, thinking of how strong Ned probably was and what sex positions they could try because he was so strong. Steve licked his lips and forced himself to be patient. He wanted to feel those muscles, that skin beckoning him before he licked it, sucked it and made love to it. But Ned had different ideas.

"You're going too slow. I'll bust a nut if you don't hurry it up!" Steve looked up and saw the teasing glint in Ned's eyes. He debated toying with Ned and going even slower, but even he didn't have enough self control for that. Plus, he wasn't an asshole.

He backed up and took off his shirt. Now it was Ned's turn to explore Steve's chest. He had a scattering of black hair on his pecs and a well defined trail to his pants. Ned ran his hands over his shoulders, kneading his shoulders and upper arms.

Even without massage oil it felt so good, so relaxing. He lowered his head forward and stretched his neck. He thought he relaxed when they left the parking lot, but his muscles were still tight and tense.

"Your hands are magic." Ned chuckled. "You don't have any massage oil by any chance, do you?" Steve chuckled. "No. I wouldn't have massage oil if I didn't have condoms."

"I'll be right back. I'm going to see what supplies the bathroom has."

Steve closed his eyes and hoped there was massage oil, or something Ned could use. He had the most magnificent hands.

Ned walked out of the bathroom smiling. "Guess what I found? A brand new massage bar!" Steve thought this was a cherry on top of the miracle of Ned being his blind date.

Ned ripped the paper off the small massage bar and rubbed the bar between his hands. Steve moaned as Ned massaged his arms. Steve was getting so relaxed now. Those hands were decadent magic. He wondered if he should lie down or if that would be too presumptuous. Steve didn't want to force Ned to give him an all body massage if he didn't want to. He didn't want to ask and make Ned not able to say no, either.

Ned tugged on his belt and Steve opened his eyes. He was staggered by the heat in Ned's eyes. Steve had never considered himself that good looking before. To see someone as hot as Ned so turned on by his body, was the best affirmation he could have ever gotten.

"Why don't I help you take these off and you can lie down on the bed. I'd be able to massage you better if you were lying down."

Steve smiled and thanked his lucky stars. He unbuckled and pulled down his pants and shorts so fast you would have thought they were on fire. Well they weren't, but he was. Hot for Ned and hot from his marvelous hands.

He finished taking off his socks and shoes and got on the bed. He laid down on his stomach as he needed his back and shoulders massaged even though he also wanted his dick massaged. Call him selfish for wanting a full body massage, but if he had a damn hot man offering you better believe he would take him up on it.

He heard clothing rustle and imagined Ned taking off the rest of his clothes. Maybe laying on his stomach wasn't the most brilliant idea he had ever had. His dick was getting harder and didn't have much room to grow in. He felt the bed dip. His anticipation made the brush of Ned's skin against his thighs that much sweeter.

Ned dug into Steve's shoulders, reaching for the places that bothered him the most. Steve moaned with sensual pleasure. He relished in the feeling of someone giving all their attention to his body.

Steve closed his eyes and focused on the fingers rubbing him, caressing his skin, digging in and making him feel so good. It was stoking his desire and need. He was burning to get release but didn't want to stop Ned. It was soothing, feeling those hands massage his back and work their way down to his ass. He couldn't wait to see what Ned would do when he got lower on his body.

Ned didn't know why he had given a massage to Steve. Other than he knew when an omega needed healing. Steve was tense and wound up from the theatrics of the morning. Sex is a great stress reliever, but Ned wanted to make Steve feel good too. The poor guy had such a shitty family and was so hot that Ned could hardly keep himself from jerking off just looking at him.

He rubbed the massage bar with his hands and scooted down Steve's body. That luscious ass was right in front of him. A nice round bubble butt. Ned put a hand on each cheek and worked his fingers into the muscles. Steve showed his appreciation by moaning long and loud.

His ass was a work of a master. So firm, yet still squishable. He wanted to put his face down and motorboat his cheeks. He controlled his desires and moved off the bed to work on a leg. Such firm, well-muscled legs. He couldn't wait to feel them around him, around his legs as he fucked Steve doggy style. His cock grew even more rigid thinking of that bubble butt pushing back against him as he pounded it. He groaned and closed his eyes.

Ned walked around the bed and started on the other leg. Steve was more relaxed and lying as if he had no muscles at all, which was what Ned wanted. He teased Steve by brushing his fingers against his balls and cock as he massaged the inner thigh. He bit back a chuckle at Steve's whining groan.

"Roll over." He was amazed at much he cared and felt protective of this omega he had just met today. Not that he was Penny's friend, or that the guy was in need. It felt right as if Steve was his omega to care for.

That brought him to an abrupt halt. There was no way he could have fallen for this omega that fast. It didn't happen that fast, did it? He wasn't sure. Ned had never found his omega before. He knew Henry and David fell hard and fast, but had to get through Henry's insecurities before they finally got together.

Ned sighed and decided that right here, right now he would focus on giving Steve the best damn massage he had ever gotten. Steve would remember this for days. Ned rubbed the massage bar on Steve's chest, which made him flinch. He rubbed it along Steve's shoulders and then down his arms.

Ned loved running his hands on Steve's muscled arms. He leaned forward and massaged Steve's face paying careful attention to his jaw, because that's where Ned had a lot of pain when he was stressed, and he could only assume Steve was the same.

Ned wanted to worship this glorious body, lavish praise on it instead of diving right into the one area that had all his attention. He forced himself to not give into temptation and suck Steve's cock. Ned ran his hands over Steve's abs and followed the treasure trail down but stopping just before hitting the pot of gold. Steve groaned with frustration.

Ned got off the bed and paid attention to the front of Steve's legs. Muscled legs turned him on, which was odd, but that's the way he was. Steve's legs were glorious, muscled and for the time being all his.

"Please put me out of my misery. Please touch me."

Steve's begging for Ned's touch ramped up his desire to a fever pitch. He wanted nothing more than to get well acquainted with that eager part of Steve's body. That part long, hard and resting on Steve's abs. He wanted Steve so desperately.

Ned finally let himself off his leash, let him have that reward for taking care of Steve's needs first. He leaned over and touched Steve's engorged cock, licking the pre-cum off the head.

Steve groaned. "Oh God, please."

Ned wrapped his hand around Steve's wide and thick cock. Lust slammed into him and he wanted to make Steve cum so hard he'd see stars for a week. Steve's cock was almost too big to fit in his mouth, but Ned was more than willing to work with a beautiful cock that big.

He couldn't hold off any longer, Ned grabbed his own cock and stroked as he sucked on Steve. Listening to Steve groan was heaven and hell. He was so happy he brought pleasure to the omega, but hell because each groan drove him closer to release, which he wouldn't do until Steve came first.

Ned worshipped that beautiful cock, running his tongue down the shaft, licking and sucking on Steve's balls. He loved the musky smell of a turned on man, he could lay his head there, breathe and be satisfied for a long time.

But he had an omega to pleasure and then finally he'd get his own release. He gave one last nuzzle to Steve's balls and then licked his way back up to the head. He wanted to show Steve how much he cared for him, how much he wanted to make Steve feel better and to see what a good alpha he was.

Ned continued to stroke himself as he ran his tongue around that big mushroom head of pleasure. Steve could barely hang on. He was tilting his hips up, grabbing onto the bedsheets and Ned's hair. Ned loved having his hair tugged during sex. Each tug went straight down to his cock. It was animalistic, primal and had him stroking faster and then squeezing his cock so he wouldn't cum. He needed to finish Steve fast or he would blow.

Ned looked at Steve, pleased to see Steve writhing and panting. "Cum for me, baby."

He took Steve's cock again and increased the speed to drive him wild. And it did. Steve screamed and stilled, shooting so hard that Ned was amazed there wasn't a hole in the roof of his mouth. He licked up every wonderful essence of Steve, savoring the taste of him. He was a treasure.

* * *

STEVE COULD BARELY THINK. He was lost in a haze of blissful pleasure, all his nerve endings recovering from a massive dose of pleasure. First a massage all over his body, lulling him into heavenly bliss and then the best blow job of his life. He was a wet noodle, his body couldn't even move. He wanted to explore Ned, run his hands and tongue all over that beautiful tanned and muscled body, but he couldn't even make his arm move.

"I can't even move." He sounded like he was drunk. Steve was drunk on endorphins. He had never felt so languid, overdosed on pleasure. Ned was a one man pleasure palace.

"Don't worry. Do you mind if I cum on you?"

Steve moaned at the thought of Ned cumming on him, marking him with his cum, as his bitch. He had never been so subservient with anyone before, but the thought of being at Ned's mercy had his cock trying to come back to life.

"So hot, love it. Do it." He'd be embarrassed at his lack of articulate speech if he hadn't seen the wide grin on Ned's face. Ned was sure pleased with his handiwork. And he should be, he was a maestro. A maestro of the dick. The cock master.

Ned straddled Steve's chest which gave him a wonderful view looking up at Ned's balls and cock with miles of bare, sculpted chest above that. Steve had died and gone to heaven. Steve would willingly be Ned's heavenly reward if he could stare at that gorgeous body. He wanted to taste that cock, those balls. Steve moaned with need. If he could have moved, he would play with his new toys right now.

"Can't move." He sounded whiny, but he didn't care. He sounded like he was being denied a toy and he was, his toy was straddling him and he couldn't move.

Ned stroked his long cock and then patted Steve's cheeks with it. Steve kept moving his head with his tongue out, trying to catch it. It was the most demented game of Whack A Mole. Ned quit teasing Steve and let him catch his cock and give it a lick.

He could feel Ned's groan of pleasure through his cock. Ned tasted delicious, like the best chocolate, coffee, cake and everything else he had denied himself. He moaned with Ned's cock in his mouth, desperate to suck that heavenly liquid.

"Oh, you feel so good. I love watching you suck on my dick."

Steve felt warmth flow through him at those words. He was embarrassed it meant so much to him, but with the day he had, any bit of praise he lapped up like a dog.

Ned pulled his cock back and Steve damn near cried. "You will make me cum if you keep that up. And I want to cum on you."

Ned reached down playing with his balls with one hand and stroking his dick with the other. His heavy breathing and moaning was shooting right to Steve's cock. Steve couldn't move his arms, and he wanted to grab Ned's thighs and squeeze them while sucking on Ned's cock. But his legs were pinning Steve's arms to his side. He could only lay back and watch the erotic show of a hot, muscled male body pleasuring himself.

Ned groaned. "I'm gunna cum!"

White lines shot out and splattered on Steve's cheeks, forehead, chin and chest. He wondered if there was something wrong with him he loved being unable to move and have Ned cum on him. The hot liquid marked him as the object of Ned's desire, the one he wanted, the one that made him crazy with lust. Steve smiled and tried to reach some cum with his tongue.

Ned collapsed on Steve, but held himself up long enough to give a quick kiss to Steve, and then roll over and collapse next to him on the bed. Steve rolled over and ran his hand down Ned's bare chest. He was getting to touch that body that had teased him and drove him to an incoherent blob on the bed. This man had skills.

He laid his chest on Ned's and listened to his heavy breathing, playing with his nipple. Steve was still a puddle of loose and relaxed muscles though one muscle was not loose and lazy anymore. He wanted more action, but he was still boneless and Ned needed time to recover. Again Steve wished he had gotten a room with a hot tub, but how was he to know his blind date would be such a fantastic man?

"Do you have any plans for the rest of today?" Ned's voice rumbled, Steve smiled as he felt the rumbles through his cheek laying on Ned's chest. He was glad to hear Ned's mind was going in the same direction his was. He wanted this day, this moment, this cocoon of safety and pleasure to last forever.

"The only plans I have are to explore your body for the rest of the day."

He ran his hand down Ned's chest to play with the curly hair next to his new favorite toy. The hairs were short and trimmed, but he still loved running his finger through them. He loved the woodsy, musk smell was that was Ned's scent. Steve breathed it in with a deep breath.

It was intoxicating. It hit his every nerve with lust. The more he played with Ned's hair, the stronger the scent became. He knew he was turning Ned on, but he was still resting, so Steve pulled his hand back and laid his arm over Ned's abs. He looked forward to exploring all of Ned the rest of the day.

*N*ed looked over at Steve, who was driving him to his car back at the park. Who would have thought his blind date would be such a hot and responsive omega? He was in love with this guy. His muscles were sore from the fun they had all day yesterday. They took many breaks to watch movies, talk and get to know each other. He hadn't had such a good time like that in longer than he could remember. Another plus was Steve's scent. It made him feel like he was at home for the holidays.

They pulled into the park's parking lot. Ned directed Steve to his car. It wasn't the only one in that lot, but it was the only one at the far end, close to the pavilion where the wedding had taken place.

"I forgot to ask you, did any relatives try to get ahold of you yesterday? It slipped my mind to ask." He smirked at Steve and winked when Steve glanced at him. Seeing Steve's smile made his cozy happiness all that stronger.

"I turned my phone off so it wouldn't bother us. I turned it back on this morning to find 14 new voicemails. I am not looking forward to listening to them."

Who would want to listen to them? "Why don't you delete the ones from the people you don't want to hear from? There's no reason to listen to all of them."

Steve looked over. "I agree, but I can't just see who called when I have my phone turned off. I have to listen to the phone number and then skip or delete. So it will be a long process but I imagine the majority are from my mother or sister. There might be some relatives I wanted to see that called. But I expect most are ones I want to delete."

"Well I hope most are from relatives that missed you and want to meet up with you."

Steve smiled and reached over for a hug. Ned patted his back and breathed in that wonderful smell of home baked holiday cookies. They pulled back and smiled at each other.

"I will be busy the rest of today, but how about getting together tomorrow?"

Steve nodded his head. "I'd like that. I'm not on call this week, so my schedule is steady and easier to plan around. Text me and we can do a dinner date or exercise date."

Ned gave him a quick kiss, then decided to hell with it and angled his head to give Steve a goodbye kiss he wouldn't forget soon. He wanted to make sure he wasn't forgotten or pushed aside by any other alpha Steve happened to run across. Ned sucked on Steve's lips, played with his tongue, and damn near humped the center console. He pulled away gratified to find Steve breathing as heavy as he was. Ned knew his eyes were full of desire for Steve, but he had to get going, plus he wanted to leave him begging for more.

"I wanted to give you a kiss so you wouldn't forget me."

Steve chuckled and ran his hand down Ned's cheek. "I'd never forget you. You took an unbearable day and made it unforgettable. And helped me get through the wedding and relatives as well."

Steve smirked and Ned smiled in response. He was glad he had helped Steve get through the day. Ned couldn't believe anyone had such horrid relatives.

"I'll text you." A quick peck on the lip and Ned got out of the car. He knew he had to leave quick before he started in on Steve and didn't want to let him go. That man could kiss.

He waved bye to Steve and walked around to the driver's side of his car. He unlocked it and sat inside. Ned started the car and then noticed a sheet under his windshield wiper. Probably some ad.

He opened the door and reached around to rip the paper out from under the wiper. He turned it over as he got back inside. It wasn't an ad. It was a plain white sheet of paper with a handwritten message.

The writing was a mess. But the message came across loud and clear. Ned chilled. He looked up and around but saw no one paying any attention. People were playing frisbee, riding their bikes or jogging. No one was near, and no one was looking his way. This had probably been left yesterday after the wedding reception.

You are a pathetic piece of shit. You should be ashamed to pervert yourself in front of God. You will go to hell and deserve it! I hope you die you faggot.

Well. He hadn't heard language like that about his being gay since middle school. Not in high school after he punched the one kid into the row of lockers. He got a suspension for it, but it was worth it. And it kept anyone else from saying what they thought. Idiots.

Ned wondered if they targeted his car since Steve's wasn't in the lot. Thank God Ned and Steve had left the reception when they did. He was glad Steve didn't have to deal with this on top of his shitty mother.

Ned narrowed his eyes. How did they know what car was his? Did they watch him pull up? That was almost creepier than the note. Someone had it out for them.

Ned crumpled up the paper and would have thrown it out of the car. If this was the first nasty message, then he would wish he had kept it for evidence. He hoped that was the end of the bullshit from he assumed Steve's mother, but if not, he had some proof it started this day.

He was also glad Steve had already taken off. He'd keep this a secret. No need to freak him out or make him worry that Ned would leave due to this harassment. He laughed. It would take a hell of a lot more to even slow him down for a second. No, he was hell bent on sticking around Steve for a long while.

"You need to do better than that, assholes." He backed up and left the parking lot. Time to go home and get some chores done. His muscles were sore, he was still in a post coital glow and had some great memories to last him till Tuesday. It was a great day.

* * *

STEVE TOOK Ned's advice and deleted any messages from his mother and sister without even listening to them. And there were a lot. He couldn't believe how they had noticed them slip out of the reception. They must have left voice mails within 10 minutes of them leaving.

If it was his wedding reception, he wouldn't have been thinking of anything except his spouse. That made him sad that his sister was so bitter she noticed when he left, but wouldn't acknowledge him or have him sit with the family. He shook his head and made plans to contact his aunt and two cousins that left messages. That left eleven messages from his mother and sister. What a family.

That taken care of, he got his scrubs together, packed his bag and made his way to work. He wasn't on call this week but had pulled the late night Sunday shift as a favor for another doctor. He didn't mind the night shift as he had no one at home that would miss him.

That used to make him feel bad, but after this weekend, that glorious day with Ned, he realized that the relationship he had just gotten out of wasn't a relationship. Sure they were together for years, but it was ho hum. Mediocre. Nothing special. They had floated on in complacency. At least it was that way for him.

He was glad that his ex had dumped him. Otherwise he would have married him at some point, not understanding that a real relationship was full of excitement, joy and a longing to be with that other person all the time. At least that's how he felt now about Ned.

He wondered if this was new relationship syndrome, but he didn't think so. They clicked. They could talk about anything, Ned was intelligent, they had a wide variety of world experiences and Ned didn't shy away from talking about anything. They were compatible in bed. He smiled again just thinking about it. This could very well be 'the one'. He was so happy.

He pulled into the doctor's reserved parking spaces at the hospital and got out. It wasn't late enough that he could only enter through the emergency entrance. He walked through the parking ramp and took the elevators to his floor. Steve wanted to study medical records and go over his plans for the surgeries he had scheduled the next day. He was a cautious guy and tended not to make any drastic moves without a lot of forethought and preparation.

Going crazy with Ned over the weekend, and by going crazy he meant holing up in a hotel for a day after just meeting the guy, was out of character for him. He decided though that being kicked out of your doldrums, out of your patterns was a good thing. It got your brain making new connections, it was revitalizing, reinvigorating and all those other words. Or maybe it was just due to the amount of great sex he had had. He smiled wickedly. And boy did Ned like to have fun. He couldn't wait till Tuesday.

He walked through the hallway smiling and waving hi at the nurses. Not too many doctors here at this hour. Unless you were on the ER or ICU floors. He went into his office and checked his email. A new surgical nurse was moving up from the night shift. They must be happy about that. You had to work for a while at the night shift before you got to move up to day shift.

Steve deleted the email. He moved on to the next house-keeping email and kept going through all his emails until he was caught up. Time to go over his plans and review medical records. He opened the files on his computer, everything was digital these days, and reviewed his plans and look over cases for later in the week.

He loved being a surgeon, helping people feel better and most times, saving their lives. Especially when other doctors misdiagnosed the problem. He settled back and prepared to be at it for a few hours. He turned on his favorite mix on Spotify and got lost in the details.

CHAPTER 8

Ned was having a great day. The day shift was tons better than the night shift. He was right in on the action from the get go, no cleanup work or emergency surgeries here. He was shadowing a day shift tech just to get a feel for the way things worked. Then after lunch he'd get his own assignments.

There were different surgeons on the day shift as well. He would miss the friends he had made working with the night crew, but they'd be on day shift before long. An opening just had to appear before that could happen though. He had paid his time waiting, and he was damn glad to have a normal day shift. Now he could get together with his friends and take on local events a lot easier.

The nurse he was shadowing didn't just give him a heads up on how things worked on the day shift, but let him know the quirks of certain nurses and surgeons. They liked things a certain way, and most surgeons were known for being arrogant, a lot likes jet pilots and attorneys he had heard. But with surgeons, with the other two he didn't know, he could understand some arrogance as they were saving lives and doing complicated work. They were playing god. And he helped them do it. Which was the draw of the job. He loved being involved in the work of saving lives and helping people. Ned didn't have the stress of being a surgeon, but had the benefits of helping.

He grabbed his wallet and headed down to the cafeteria for lunch. It was packed. A real lunch hour with daylight and people! Ned chuckled. Sunlight! He had waited a long time for this. An elbow to the side got his attention.

"Before I forget, make sure you stick by the rule of no dating within the department. We lost a good surgical tech due to that."

Ned looked over with interest at the nurse he was shadowing. She was no nonsense but had passed along some helpful tidbits of info and this was one he was interested in.

"Really?"

"Yeah, there are more people on the day shift, more surgeries so they lay the hammer down on it during the day. It was different on the nights, I was there myself, but don't cross that line now."

"I don't plan on it. I don't know anyone on day shift, so it won't be a problem. Plus, I've got someone I'm seeing, anyway."

He wondered if Steve knew he was Ned's now. He should probably make that clear on Tuesday, the day they had planned for their next date. If you could consider that disaster of a wedding a date. He wasn't sure to count the hotel room as a date. But they got to know each other during it. So, he guess it would count as a date. A prolonged and pleasurable fuck fest is what he'd call it.

He picked out a salad, he didn't just talk the talk, but he walked the walk as a health professional, and made his way to a table. What a difference some daylight made. The cafeteria was bright with sunlight, the plants looked more alive and people were talking.

At night it was full of those waiting for people in emergency surgeries or in the ICU. Not the happiest of events, so it was solemn filled with some conversation about how they were praying for someone to pull through. He had always felt like he was intruding or being rude just sitting at a table and eating while reading a book.

"So, do you have questions?"

He shook his head. "No, you've been great. Especially with the details about the different surgeons. That will help me out."

"No problem."

They focused on eating for a while. Hospital cafeterias weren't known for having great food, but the chef salad wasn't too bad. He wished they had more of a selection of salad dressings, but he'd survive.

He was looking around the room when he spotted a familiar profile and snapped his eyes back. It was Steve, it had to be! He'd know that black hair and profile anywhere with all the time he had spent with him in close contact Saturday. He didn't know Steve worked at this hospital. He hoped he was in a different department than his or they'd run into trouble before they had barely started their relationship.

"I have a question now, if you don't mind."

"No that's ok, go ahead."

Ned rolled his lips, thinking of how to phrase it, and hoping the other nurse wasn't one to gossip. "What if you were in a relationship with someone, but didn't know they worked at the same hospital?"

At the nurse's look of disbelief Ned clarified. "It's a very new relationship, we knew our jobs but not where. I didn't know he worked here."

His mentor took a drink of her coffee and looked pensive. "I don't know what to tell you. I don't think you can get grand-fathered in. I would keep it a secret and hope you don't get found out. One of you would have to move to a different department if that was the case or move before you get found out. That would be the best option."

Ned nodded and looked down. He liked none of those ideas. He rather liked seeing Steve every day, at work and the possibility of working with him. But he could see manage-ment's point, if things went south or if a couple were fighting and not professional. It could be a bad deal for the patients and coworkers. He took a drink of coffee and would see how things went before he got all worked up about it.

"So, new relationship?"

Ned smiled. "Yeah, very new. Very awesome too. I don't want to give it up."

"Well then, take my advice and hold onto it. It's rare that you connect with someone, especially someone that you think you can take on the long haul. They are worth their weight in gold."

They toasted with their styrofoam cafeteria cups. "Isn't that the truth?"

He couldn't wait to continue exploring this relationship with Steve. He was sure Steve was the one for the long haul.

* * *

STEVE GOT UP, emptied his tray and moved to the exit of the cafeteria. He could eat in his office, but he liked to get out when he could. Not that eating in the hospital cafeteria was getting out. But, at least it was away from his work, the smells, the people in the waiting room, the conference rooms where he hoped to not have to break bad news.

Steve shook himself and made his way to the stairs. He was like most doctors here in the hospital, they avoided the elevators and used the stairs. Any way to keep that body in shape and stave off disease and the symptoms of old age. Speaking of old age that weekend invigorated him. He smiled as he thought of Ned, the hot as hell alpha that had rocked his world on Saturday. Steve couldn't wait to see him again.

He couldn't believe he had spent one full day with Ned and already all of his past relationships had paled in comparison. There had never been the connection, the feeling of being free to share any thoughts, to discuss anything that came up, to share their inner desires and secret things they wanted to try out.

Ned was a find. He should send Penny a huge flower bouquet as a thank you. She came through for him. He had never called on her for such a big favor before, but he knew if anyone could help him out at the last minute, it would be her. David wasn't paying her enough. Or maybe he was, and that's why she stuck around?

Steve walked out the door onto his floor and went to his office. He pulled up the records of the patients he would see this afternoon and of the surgeries for tomorrow. He was intent on studying an MRI when there was a knock at his door.

"Come in." He was curious, he didn't get people that knocked and waited. They either gave a knock and opened the door or didn't bother and came right in. That last one was a pet peeve of his. It irritated him to no end.

It was the mail service. The student entered with a package and then closed the door. He wasn't expecting anything. He grabbed the big envelope from the corner of his desk and sat back down. There was no return address which was odd. He stilled, wondering if he should even open this. Who would send him something with no return address?

His curiosity got the better of him and he opened the envelope. It was one piece of paper, a letter hand written. Oh my God, what nut job is this? He had never gotten hate mail or crazy mail, but he knew other doctors had. He looked at the hand writing and could decipher the cursive enough to make it out.

Steve,

You are no longer welcome at any relative gatherings any more. You are an embarrassment to the family and are despicable. You have no shame. You ran out on your sister's wedding after being gone for a long time with your 'date' doing ungodly things. Do not ever contact us.

(Signed) Janet Wilder

Holy. Shit. His own mother was the nut job. His own mother. He had kept his home address a secret and so now she was going after him where he worked. He raised his head to the ceiling and closed his eyes. Why couldn't he have been born into a normal family? He rubbed his forehead as he felt a headache coming on.

Steve shook his head wondering what he could do about this. He wanted her to leave him alone. It was funny though, she made a big deal about his showing up for his sister, and then after she berated him in front of the entire table, he left early and gets berated for leaving early. You couldn't win with her.

He wondered if she would do anything else. Steve didn't want to alert anyone in management about this crazy letter because A) it was his own mother and B) he didn't know if it would continue. If this was it, great, he'd bury it in his desk. If it wasn't, well then he had this letter.

Decision made, he put the letter and envelope in his desk drawer, but under other things so he didn't have to look at it. What a complete nut job. He did not understand why his mother was that crazy. He felt sorry for his sister that did not understand how nuts their mother was and went along with all of it. He felt for her husband. Did he know the level of crazy he had just married into?

He was glad that his mother went after him and not Ned. He was sure Ned wouldn't get scared off by any crazy letter his mother would write, anyway. Hell, he'd probably send it back with spelling corrections. Steve laughed and took a drink of his water. He felt better already. Even just thinking about Ned had him calmed down, peaceful and ready to get back to work and focus on what was important.

$\mathcal{N}$ed got all the tools ready for the surgeon. This was his second full day of working as a surgical nurse on the day shift. He had met a lot of of the surgeons, and all were great to work for. More brusque than others, but all were fine. He was enjoying being able to get home and see some sunlight. Ned finished getting everything laid out, checked his sheet again for the surgery and went in the prep room just outside the OR or operating room.

He never looked to see what surgeon he would be paired with until he had his basic prep done. Then he would do additional prep or move things around depending on what he knew about the surgeon. This one would be with Dr. Wilder. He hadn't worked with him yet, so he left everything the way it was. He put his face mask down so the surgeon could see his face before they went in.

The other nurses and techs were familiar with each other, having been on the day shift for several years already. That's how often a day shift position opened. When one finally did, it was like winning a gold medal or the lottery.

More people for this surgery piled into the prep room, getting ready and gathering around. Ned was busy talking to an anesthesiologist he had struck up a friendship with when the surgeon told everyone to listen up. That voice sounded familiar.

Ned looked over and couldn't help his mouth from dropping open. It was Steve! He blinked as he realized that he should have recognized that last name, but he hadn't put the pieces together until he saw Steve, or Dr. Wilder. Wow. Ned would work with his squeeze. He put his memories of Steve's body out of his mind and paid attention to what Steve was saying. Ned didn't want to get in trouble his first week up on day shift. What would happen if they were found to be dating?

Ned smacked himself and was glad he had his serious face on when Steve glanced over and then did a double take. Ned pretended like he did not understand what was going on and kept his focus on Steve's throat. After a few seconds Steve talked again. He blinked and knew that his fellow surgery attendants would know something was up between them. As long as they didn't know they were in a relationship, things would be fine.

A bad feeling dropped into Ned's stomach as he wondered if this would throw Steve off too much to do the surgery. He felt bad, but he didn't know that Steve worked at this hospital. Ned wondered if he should have figured that out, but then decided that was too much. He had only met the guy on Saturday. They didn't even say where they worked. What were the odds they would be at the same hospital? There were many surgery centers and other hospitals in the area. The odds were unbelievable that they were both here in the same hospital and same department. Oh well, there was nothing to be done for it now.

Steve handled everything with the surgery prep meeting. It was informative and just what they needed. Ned nodded to let Steve know that he understood the instructions. He masked up and went into the OR. Time for the fun to begin. Ned put Steve and anything else out of his mind except for what he needed to know for this surgery. They were doing an appendectomy which was routine these days, but sometimes they had surprises with them. At least on day shift he probably wouldn't have to deal with any emergency surgery of ruptured appendixes. Those were a pain. This one would be laparoscopic and probably quick since the appendix was only inflamed and not yet ruptured. Easy peasy.

* * *

STEVE LEFT the OR satisfied with a job well done. He washed up, changed, so he wasn't wearing blood, and went down the hall to meet with the patient's parents. It was a quick and fast talk, everything went fine, no surprises, short surgery, easy and fast recovery, thanks bye. Those were the best surgeries. With young patients like teens, they had the best recovery rates. Those always were the preferred patients.

Now it was time to deal with the huge surprise he got right before surgery. Ned was a surgical nurse at his hospital! He was staggered, but he didn't show it in the prep meeting. He laughed to himself as he thought of the odds. How would they both end up at the same place? Who knew?

He had been here for years so he had that going in their favor if anyone from the surgical team thought to bring it up to management. Hopefully no one would. They had nothing to go on, just that he recognized Ned. There was no way to tell that they were dating. The others could think they were past roommates or something. Who knows? He wasn't saying anything that was for sure.

The problem he had to deal with now was the typical one all surgeons had after surgery. Especially if they were male. He was horny as hell. Steve walked down the hallway wondering where he could go for a quick jack off. He knew from stories that surgeons weren't the only ones with this issue. Anyone that dealt with high stress and adrenaline had an overload of horniness after the stressful event. He wanted to find Ned and see if he wanted to help him out, but he also didn't want to have anyone see them together.

Steve ran his hand through his hair. What a dilemma. He might as well go to his old standby of either trying to get calmed down by running up and down the stairs or by going into a stall and jacking off. Steve went for the stairs. He walked down the hallway and looked at his watch. Noting the time and how much time he had for his 'recovery session' he opened the stairwell door and jogged down. His floor was on 5th, so he had a few floors to go down, and then back up. Just once down and up cured him of any horniness. But it always depended on the day, the surgery that came before, the stress of anything he had to deal with.

He jogged down to 1st floor without running into anyone. One time he was so focused on himself that he almost ran into a surgeon and nurse on the 3rd floor landing going right at it. He threw himself against the wall, passed them and kept on jogging. It was well known among hospital staff that male surgeons will have an excess of adrenaline that needed to get worked off. No one had made any complaints, so nothing was ever done. He didn't know if management just ignored it or if they knew... they had to know. It was an open secret in the medical world.

Steve turned around on 1st and started his jog back up. He wished Ned was here right now. What he wouldn't give to get a hand job and a good fucking right now. He circled up around 2nd and almost ran into someone jogging down the stairs. He saw feet, moved over to the right as he looked up.

Speak of the devil, it was Ned. A huge smile erupted on his face. Ned looked like Christmas had come early for him too.

"I was just jogging off some... adrenaline. How about you?"

Ned stepped down, so they were on the same step as each other. He smelled divine, the musky wood scent going straight to his cock, making it even harder than it already was. He squeezed his cock through his scrubs and groaned.

"You're killing me. I was jogging hoping to undo this hard on and you made it a thousand times worse."

Ned scooted closer and leaned over, licking a trail from his scrubs to in front of his ear.

"Oh I am, am I?" Ned was killing him. He wrapped his hand around Steve's cock and squeezed. Then he shoved his hands down Steve's scrubs and grabbed ahold of him. Steve leaned back against the wall and groaned. He had to keep quiet, Steve wanted no one hear them, but my God, how could he keep it quiet?

"You're so fucking hot. I love seeing you at my mercy, all your clothes on with your cock hanging out in my hand. Look at that, you're dripping already. I bet you'd like a hand with that, wouldn't you?"

Ned was leaning against the wall, leaning on one arm above Steve's head and the other still stroking him for all he was worth. Steve almost didn't care if the entire staff of the 5th floor walked down the steps right now. He would beg for Ned not to stop. This was so much better than jogging it off, or taking care of it by himself in the bathroom.

Steve reached down in Ned's pants. Ned's cock was hard and dripping. He smiled thinking of taking Ned in his mouth. They stroked each other looking in each other's eyes. Ned leaned in and pressed his lips to Steve's and Steve was off in the best living daydream ever of the cold concrete wall against his back and the hot hand stroking his cock. The hot lips, stubble scratching his face, the tongue wrapping around his, his hand on Ned's cock, he was adrift in pleasure, over-whelmed with sensations. He was going to cum fast.

Ned pulled back and took his hand off Steve's cock. Steve opened his eyes in shock. "What are you doing?" He needed to cum right now!

Ned leaned in to give him a peck and a quick squeeze that had Steve moaning again.

"I want to do something a little more than just jack each other off."

Anything was fine with Steve, anything at all. He desired Ned so bad that one lick on his cock and he'd embarrass himself cumming. Ned just did that to him though. He wanted to be at Ned's mercy, have him call the shots, tell him what to do. Steve couldn't wait.

Ned pulled at his scrub top, pulled him to stand up and then positioned Steve in front of the railing at the inside of the stairwell. He could look down to the basement floor. Steve wrapped his hands on the cold railing and looked back. Ned had pulled his scrub pants down and was putting a condom on.

Steve's eyebrows rose. "You will fuck me, here?" He looked up and down, his earlier thought anything would be ok wasn't the case when he was confronted with getting fucked in plain view of anyone in the stairwell.

"We're both so hard, it will be fast and furious. I've got lube and a condom. Don't worry, I won't put you in any pain. I'll take care of you."

That warmed his heart, hearing an alpha say they would take care of him, but still. This was risky. He stopped thinking when he felt Ned's finger in his ass. In and out, in and out, Ned was moving it around and then pulled it out. Steve whined, but two fingers soon pushed past his muscles to move around. The pleasure was amazing, indescribable, just what he wanted. Steve moaned, reached down and stroked his own cock. He was going to cum so fast at this rate. Ned's fingers were magic, the conductor's wand of this symphony of pleasure.

Ned pulled his fingers out and Steve whined again. He heard Ned chuckle behind him and then felt the large head of Ned's cock. Oh yes! He pushed back, eager to get that monster dick in his ass. This was one position they hadn't tried on Saturday. Standing almost straight up. Steve leaning over the railing with one foot on the step below. It was an odd position, but Ned was right there with him.

Steve held on to the railing with one hand and kept stroking his dick with the other, rubbing his hand over the head using his pre-cum as lube. Steve wasn't even paying attention to his own dick, but more on the sensation of Ned behind him, his hand on his hip, Ned's dick pushing past his muscles, stroking in and out. Oh God! He bent his head back and lost himself in the sensation.

Both of Ned's hands were now on his hips. He felt the hair on Ned's legs rubbing against his thighs. Ned picked up the pace, moving in and out faster. This angle was perfect for hitting his prostate and Ned was a master of Steve's body, already. The orgasm was pulling out of him, coming from deep in his legs, shooting out of his dick. Steve clenched his teeth to keep quiet but his groan was long. Ned grabbed the hair at the back of his head, longer than he liked it, but enough for Ned to grab. He loved that feeling of being at Ned's mercy, fucked against a railing, pushed against it, surrounded by Ned's body, his dick, his hand, his arm. Ned leaned hard against Steve's back as he jerked and rode through his orgasm. Fuck that was the best fuck he'd ever had. Hotter than anything they had done on Saturday.

He leaned over the railing panting, his hand covered with his cum resting on the railing. Ned leaned against his back, resting his head on Steve's back. That was a hell of a fuck. He hoped no one ever found out they were seeing each other. Having Ned help him with his post surgery hard on problem was a lot better and a lot more fun than taking care of it himself.

Steve felt Ned's lips on his upper back, where his scrubs had been pulled down during the festivities.

"You were fucking amazing, Steve. I love how responsive you are, how beautiful your ass is. You were so hot."

Steve smiled and looked back at Ned.

"You weren't so bad yourself." He wiggled his ass and chuckled as Ned's eyes almost rolled back from pleasure. He pulled out of Steve and then smacked his ass. The sharp smacking sound loud and unexpected enough to make Steve jump. Ned laughed and massaged Steve's butt cheek.

"Sorry, I couldn't resist. I love your bubble butt."

Steve turned around and shook his head at him. "Do you happen to have any napkins or Kleenex in that magic pocket of yours? I'm covered in spoo."

CHAPTER 10

The last few weeks had flown by. They had kept their relationship a secret so far. The other members of the surgical team had wondered about Steve's obvious recognition of Ned, which they passed off as having known each other from Ned's interning. There were no repercussions of their stairwell session either, and they recreated it a few more times.

Ned was having the most fun he'd ever had. Steve was fun, a great conversationalist, intelligent which was a given since he was a surgeon, and pleasant to be around when they were just reading or lounging on the weekend.

Ned put another handful of popcorn in his mouth. The movie they had been watching was on pause while Steve was in the bathroom. Everything was going so well that Ned wondered if something bad would happen. It wasn't like him to think things like this, but he had heard nothing from Steve about wedding repercussions and he was sure there had been some. He didn't want to bring it up though. If Steve needed help, or wanted to talk, then he could bring it up. Ned would not bring up a topic that was unpleasant and had more bad feelings for Steve than Ned.

Ned wondered what was going on with Steve though. He had been going to the bathroom a lot more. Steve shouldn't have diabetes as he was in perfect health and fit as Ned could attest to. He smiled as he chewed his popcorn, thinking back on the fun they had earlier that evening. Steve had wanted to try out some things he found online since Ned was so willing to try new things. Ned felt bad for the guy that he had had such shitty alphas before, but not everyone was as fun as he was. Plus, it's not like he wasn't getting anything out of the experimentation. He was getting laid and pleasing his omega at the same time. A big win in his book.

Ned paused mid chew and realized that he thought of Steve as his omega. He thought about it and realized he didn't feel scared or like running out the door. Ned was fine and rather pleased with the thought. He smiled even bigger and kept chewing. His omega. Steve, his omega. He liked the sound of that. He couldn't wait for Steve to get out here so he could bring up moving in together.

Ned looked at the clock and realized it had been about 20 minutes already. There was something going on here. Ned put the popcorn bowl down and went back down the hallway to the bathroom. He knocked on the door.

"Steve? Is everything ok in there?"

He felt like he was too overprotective, that there was nothing wrong, that he was butting in and making Steve uncomfortable. He grimaced.

"I'm sorry, Steve. I was concerned because I noticed you had to go a lot and I thought maybe you were sick or something. I'm sorry to... butt in." He turned around to walk back to the living room, feeling like an idiot when he heard the door open. He turned back around and stopped at the look on Steve's face.

Steve looked pale, like he was sick, yet he also had a small smile, proud yet unsure. It was quite a mix of emotions playing across Steve's face. Something was going on. He took one of Steve's hands and held it, rubbing his thumb on the back of Steve's hand. Ned waited for Steve to say something. He had already asked what was wrong, so he would not say it again. Steve would pipe up when he was ready.

Steve ran his hand through his hair and then smiled at Ned shaking his head.

"Well, I have some news."

Ned kept hold of Steve's hand and waited. And waited. Maybe he needed a push to get it out.

"I'm right here. Whatever is wrong, we'll get through it together."

Steve laughed and put his hand on Ned's shoulder.

"Funny you should say... I've been running to the bathroom a lot because I've been nauseous."

Ned just looked at Steve and kept rubbing his hand. It was probably more to calm Ned down than to help Steve out in any way. Steve laughed and closed his eyes. He opened them again and Ned was feeling relieved at the happy look in Steve's eyes. It couldn't be cancer or anything with a look like that.

"I took a pregnancy test. And another. And another. We're having a baby."

What? Ned stopped everything and just stared at Steve. He only realized his mouth was open when his tongue was getting dry. And then he realized that he had left Steve hanging, on a pregnancy announcement. Oh God, that was not good.

"I'm just... speechless! Wow! Congratulations!" He wrapped Steve up in a big hug. He was still too shocked to be coherent at this point. Wow, a dad. He would be a dad. Wow.

He pulled back and looked at Steve. "How long have you known? Did you suspect today? Were you taking pregnancy tests tonight? Is that why you were going to the bathroom a lot? Are you ok? Are you happy? I mean I congratulated you but what if you're not happy?"

Steve laughed and put a finger on Ned's lips to stop him from talking.

"I love you Ned. It may be too early for that declaration, but I've known it for a while now and your cute nonstop running at the mouth questions proved it. You were concerned for me, thinking of me first and not yourself. That's an alpha I want."

Ned was so overcome that tears welled up in his eyes. He pulled Steve in for another tight hug. Ned rubbed his omega's back, rocking back and forth, laying his head against Steve's. He couldn't believe it. He would be a dad. What a day!

Ned pulled back again. "How far along are you? Can you tell this soon? When did you think you were pregnant?"

Steve shut him up with a finger on his mouth again. Ned took that finger in his mouth and sucked. Heat flared in Steve's eyes and it matched the heat in Ned's eyes. Ned knew nothing hotter. His omega carrying his baby was a hell of an aphrodisiac. Ned felt like running outside, screaming to the world that he knocked up Steve. He giggled and then bent over laughing. It had to be due to the shock of the unexpected announcement from Steve.

"Are you ok there, Ned? You're punchy."

Ned nodded his head and held up a hand. He'd get control over himself at some point. He took a few deeps breaths and then ran his hands through his hair.

"What a day. We need to celebrate. Are you up for celebrating?"

Steve raised an eyebrow. "How were you thinking of celebrating? I won't drink any alcohol, and I'm nauseous right now so any fun times will have to be postponed."

Ned wrapped Steve in a hug and then propelled him back to the living room.

"I think we can celebrate by having you cuddle up next to me, with the popcorn bowl and a nice hot cup of tea. I'll get that mint tea that you've been drinking. How does that sound?"

"It sounds perfect. Thank you."

Ned leaned over and gave Steve a slow, sensual kiss. His omega, pregnant with his child. Ned was bowled over with excitement. He would be a dad!

* * *

AT THE HOSPITAL, Steve came out of the bathroom stall and washed his hands. He dried them, stood up straight and walked out the door like he hadn't just puked up his guts in there. No one else had been in the bathrooms each time he needed to puke this week, but he was afraid his luck would run out. He didn't know what the hospital policy was on pregnant doctors, especially surgeons who needed steady hands and needed not to be running out of the operating rooms puking. Steve would get back to his office and look it up.

Steve passed colleagues and nodded his head and smiled. He missed the post surgery rendezvous with Ned. Since he had been nauseous almost around the clock, they hadn't had sex. Steve didn't know about Ned, but he was missing it despite feeling the need to puke. He sighed and wondered how long this morning, night, around the clock sickness would last. Steve didn't enjoy this one bit.

He got to his office and sat down. Steve pulled another ginger ale out of his mini fridge and cracked it open. Ah. That felt wonderful. He felt so lucky to have such a good alpha in Ned. He kept Steve's fridge stocked with ginger ales. Steve had never seen him come in, but every day there were ginger ales like Steve had never even taken one out. Ned was good.

Steve took another sip and sat back. Time to find his hospital policy handbook and see what they said. He grabbed the binder off the shelves behind him and opened it up. Steve found the section marked pregnancy in the policy book and flipped to that section. He sat back and read. The language was boring legalese watered down for non lawyers, but it was still horrible and he wished there was an English translation. He was not going to Human Resources to just ask them what their policy was. They would want to know who the dad was, and that would lead to some awkward silences or lies on his part. He was the worst liar ever, and he didn't want to get in trouble lying to HR. Steve sighed and wished everything would work out with no problems. That would be nice.

Ah, here it was. He was a surgeon so according to the policy, he could still practice as long as he wasn't experiencing any side effects that would make it dangerous for the patient. Steve's hands were still steady so that was good. Also he could sit down when operating so that would still be ok. As long as he could reach over his belly, he could still work. So it looked like he'd have to go on leave when his belly got too big. That sounded all good to him.

Relieved, Steve downed the rest of the ginger ale and made a 3 point shot right into the trash can. Things would be just fine. There was quick double knock at the door and then Ned peeked his head in.

"Are you busy?"

Steve shook his head. "No, what's up?"

"Nothing. I wanted to see my favorite omega."

Ned came around the desk and leaned down for a quick kiss. Steve loved that Ned would pop in checking on him. He loved the feeling of Ned's arms on him, the musky woody scent that Ned always had. Steve felt comfortable and at peace every time he smelled it.

Ned pulled back and sat on the edge of Steve's desk. "How are you doing today? Has the nausea gone away yet?"

Steve shook his head. "Not yet. I just puked again. Don't worry, I rinsed my mouth out with mouthwash."

Ned grimaced and then tried to smile. It was ridiculous.

"I shouldn't be grossed out, I mean we swap fluids often, but there's something about puke that just... grosses me out."

Steve laughed. "No problem. It grosses me out too. Thank God I'm not a nurse. I don't know how they deal with all of that crap. You couldn't pay me enough."

"Me either. What do you think you'd feel up for with dinner? I could make chicken noodle soup or we could be at your place? We should do something about that, having two places is ridiculous."

"I didn't want to push you into anything."

Ned gave him a look. Steve shrugged and tried not to feel like he was a child in trouble.

"You couldn't push me into anything. We're having a child together. I love you. It's time we moved in."

Steve smiled and chuckled. Ned did not beat around the bush. He was all straight forward, ready to get shit done. It was refreshing considering the bullshit he had to put up with when dealing with his mother. Emotional blackmail, guilt trips and made up sob stories didn't even cover it.

"Ok, let's talk more tonight about it. I'll meet you at your car. What time do you think you'll be done?

Ned looked at his watch and then thought for a few seconds. "I think I can get out by 5:30. That sound good? I'll meet you at the car at 5:40."

Ned leaned over and gave Steve a quick peck and then walked out of the office. Steve sighed. One of these days, when he wasn't puking, he would get Ned to fuck him over his desk. He had always wanted to do that. Steve sighed and rubbed his stomach. First things first though, he had to get over this nausea. It was driving him up a wall.

CHAPTER 11

Ned put the dry pasta into the boiling water and then checked on the rest of the soup in the other pot. All looked good. He grabbed a spoon and took a taste. It need more spices and garlic for his taste, but it was probably fine for Steve. He didn't want to make Steve feel any worse. Ned put the spoon in the sink and dried his hands.

He turned around and looked at the now very crowded living room. They not only needed a bigger place, they needed to get a house together. They both had been in apartments, and with Ned's being bigger and closer to the hospital, they had Steve move in here.

Ned's bicycle was leaning against the wall in the living room. Video game consoles were surrounding the TV. It was a mess. A lot of boxes were still in Ned's garage. They didn't have to get everything moved out; they had a week left before Steve had to move out. But they both wanted it done as soon as possible. They didn't want to spend another second apart.

Ned wondered if any of his friend's knew a good real estate agent. They needed to find a bigger place to live sooner rather than later. Steve hadn't showed yet, but Ned wanted to be in a bigger place before he did. He didn't want Steve to hurt himself trying to lift and move boxes with a baby bump. He knew Steve would do it too. He wouldn't let anyone do all the work for him. He loved that about Steve, but it was hard to deal with when he was trying to protect Steve and the baby.

Steve came out of the bedroom tearing down a cardboard box.

"Well, that's another box done. I shoved my clothes in the empty drawers in your chest. There wasn't much room in your closet but I added what I could fit in there. We need to find a bigger place."

Ned laughed. "That's what I was just thinking. We need to find one fast."

Steve nodded his head and threw the cardboard box on the pile near the door.

"What's for dinner?"

Steve walked over for a hug. Ned held him rocking back and forth, rubbing his back. He loved the feeling of holding someone that loved you back. It was the best feeling in the world. Steve's natural scent of nutmeg and holiday spices also made him feel at home.

"I'm making chicken noodle soup. Is that ok for dinner? Or should we order in?"

Steve said nothing, he just laid his head down on Ned's shoulder.

"I could fall asleep standing up like this. I am so comfortable."

Ned kissed Steve's head and kept rubbing his back. He knew that pregnancy caused tiredness, but Ned hadn't expected this much. They rocked back and forth for a while. Ned wasn't sure if Steve was still awake, and he was loath to move him to the couch and wake him up. So he just rocked around in a circle, like a middle school dance all over again. He smiled at that, wondering how cute Steve must have looked in middle school. Some kids looked good at that age, but Ned knew had hadn't been one of them. Braces, acne and glasses were not Ned's friend during that time.

He slowly moved to the couch but Steve woke up when Ned quit rocking them.

"I think I fell asleep."

"I wasn't sure if you had or not. I was just going to move you to the couch, so you'd be more comfortable."

Steve yawned and rubbed his eyes, then ran his hands down his face. "I should probably stay awake so I can sleep tonight. Did we ever figure out what we were doing for dinner?"

Ned shook his head. Steve was so adorable with his hair sticking up on one side and still sleepy. "Let me tuck you in the couch and I'll bring you the chicken noodle soup off the stove."

Steve yawned again and let himself get led over to the couch. Ned tucked him in with a blanket. His phone rang just then. Ned picked up his phone. He was getting a call from Henry.

"Hey, how are you doing?"

"I'm doing great! I haven't seen you for a while, I've been busy with the new baby."

Ned smiled, and he swore his chest puffed out as he thought of his own news. "Speaking of baby... my partner and I are expecting!"

"Ah, that's terrific! Congratulations! When are you due?"

"Not sure yet, it's still in the very early stages. We've moved into my place and are looking for a bigger place. So if you hear of anything let me know."

"Will do. I'm so happy for you, I can't believe it, another baby!"

Ned smiled and turned to stare at Steve on the couch. He had fallen asleep and was looking adorable.

"Yeah, I can't believe it either, but it's perfect." He felt so much love for Steve, he was surprised his heart wasn't bursting out of his chest.

"I was calling because David and I will have a small gathering at our place Saturday afternoon. We want you to be there. It starts at 3 PM."

"Ok, I think we can make it. I'll check with Steve when he wakes up. Is it the standard BYOB?"

"No, this is a little different. We'll supply everything. We just want you to show up and be there." That sounded... odd. Ned wondered what was going on. Was it a baptism, but didn't that happen in a church? Ned frowned trying to figure out, but he couldn't think of anything. Maybe a moving in celebration? New baby party?

"No problem."

"Great, see you then. I've got to go, more phone calls to make."

Ned put the phone down and wondered if Henry and David were getting married Saturday. It would be just like Henry to have a small, informal wedding like that. He wouldn't want a huge event, just small with family. The more Ned thought about it, the more he realized he was probably right. He'd have to bring a gift, but a few days wasn't a big head start. He'd think of something.

* * *

STEVE SWIGGED MORE ginger ale and put the can in his locker space. He took off his dirty scrubs and threw them in the opening for soiled clothing. Lord he was glad he didn't have to do the laundry around here. How gross would that job be? He stepped in the shower and washed himself off. He hadn't felt horny after a surgery since he got pregnant. It's like his hormones took a nose dive since he was already knocked up, so why bother coming out to play. He snorted and knew it was a ridiculous analogy. He knew once you got pregnant your libido took a nose dive until the middle of the pregnancy.

He shut off the shower and toweled himself off. Steve was showing now, the baby bump was still small, but with his 6 pack of abs, it was apparent he was pregnant. He smiled and shook his head, still amazed at the turn of events. Steve found his alpha and got pregnant all thanks to his sister's wedding. He wondered if she would appreciate a thank you card. Steve laughed and decided that would be pushing it.

He got dressed in new scrubs, put his shoes on and headed out. Steve made his way up to his office and pulled off the sticky note on the door. His stomach dropped. Come see Bob M.? What in the hell? He couldn't think of any reason for this note. He knew Bob was in HR, but why leave a sticky note and not an email? Unless he knew Steve didn't go through his emails until after his work day ended and Bob had something that needed to be addressed sooner. Steve crumpled up the note and threw it in his trash can. Well, might as well go now since he had time.

* * *

STEVE WALKED into the HR offices and found Bob right away. Bob waved him in and told him to close the door. Oh boy. Steve sat down and tried to relax. No one should know about them, they had been very careful. He wondered if the no intradepartmental dating was the problem here or if something else had gone on. He decided to not say anything and wait to see what Bob had.

"I'm sorry to call you down here, but this couldn't wait. Uh, we got a letter in the mail today, pertaining to you."

Steve frowned trying to imagine what patient would write what had to be a negative letter. He thought back over the past several months and couldn't think of anytime in which his patient was not satisfied with their surgery. He could not for the life of him, figure out what was going on.

"It's... odd. I want you to read it."

Steve leaned forward and took the letter from Bob's hand. It was a normal looking letter, but when he read it, he paled and then got furious. He wanted to crumple it up, burn it, stomp on it, call his mother and scream at her. How dare she! How dare she try to ruin his life like this!

"I can see by your reaction you've read the entire letter. I must admit I was shocked that your mother would write something like this. Have you been having problems with her and... as HR I can't ask questions but I wonder if your mother has been diagnosed yet?"

Which was a nice way of saying his mother was bat shit crazy. That he already knew. He shook his head and chewed on the inside of his cheek. He wanted to stand up and pace, pull his hair, scream but he was stuck in this chair in HR so he had to stay calm and calm himself down. That psychotic cow. He didn't know what else he could do. Get a restraining order? Who got a restraining order against their mother?

"Yes, that's my mother and yes, it comes as a surprise. I didn't know she would stoop that low to go after me where I worked. She's been like this my entire life. Calling professors in college, calling roommates to ask what time I went to bed, etc." As Steve was talking, Bob's eyebrows hit his hairline and his eyes got wider.

"I know, it sounds unreal, like no one could be this crazy outside an institution, but I swear to you, it is all true and I have references to all events you could call. The professors she contacted, my roommates, my past relationships, all of it. I am surprised she's this upset about me cutting her out of my life."

Steve stopped and ran his hand through his hair. He wished he had ginger ale to drink right now. He felt like puking.

"So you cut her out of your life?"

Steve nodded his head. "Yes. At my sister's wedding several weeks ago. Before that I wouldn't let her know my home address because she'd stop without notice too many times and it was hard to get her to leave without rearranging my cabinets. I'm serious, ask my exes. She is something else.

Anyway, she confronted me at the reception when my date and I were sitting at our table. Then my date and I snuck out early so she couldn't start in on me after most of the guests had left."

Steve ran his hands down his face and shook his head. What an ordeal. "Oh, also I got a letter mailed here from her. I kept it in my desk drawer in my office."

Bob frowned. "Why didn't you tell us?"

"Because it's embarrassing when it's your mother doing the harassing. And I hoped that was the only thing she would do. Turns out I was optimistic."

Bob sighed. "If you could bring that down, we'll make a copy of it. But what she says in the letter, not the homophobic ranting, but you're dating someone from work? Is that true?"

And here it comes. Steve was so mad. This would not only affect him, but now his alpha, Ned. Damn her. She didn't want him to ever be happy, did she?

"Yes. He was my blind date to the wedding as I needed one last minute. We hit it off and didn't realize we both worked here until the next week." He hoped Bob didn't ask how that was possible. Steve didn't want to tell the guy they were busy with other things than talking.

"I cannot believe your mother is the one behind this, but she signed her name, and with your admission of her past behavior and another letter you received... I'm sorry you have to deal with this."

Steve nodded his head. He wanted to cry now. Steve went from being so irate he could light fires with his eyes, to wanting to curl up in a ball and cry. Crazy pregnancy hormones. He wished Ned was here. On second thought, he was glad Ned was not. This was embarrassing and hard enough for him to get through, but to drag Ned into it? Beyond embarrassing. What if he decided Steve was too much of a pain with his mother this way? Now Steve was tearing up.

Bob was looking at him. It looked like today was the day for revelations.

"I'm not normally so emotional. I would like you to keep this quiet, but I'm pregnant."

Bob was surprised. He congratulated Steve and then asked is his mother knew.

"No. And I don't want to even think of what she would do if she found out. I don't know if I can get a restraining order against her. Or even if I could get a psych eval to stick when only one of her kids thinks she needs one."

Bob's eyebrows couldn't go any higher. "My sister is almost like her. She sees mother as overprotective but nothing crazy. Mom hasn't done her crazy crap with my sister, and whenever she rips into me, it's not with anyone from my immediate family around."

Bob sighed and shocked his head. "What a kettle of fish. Well, you are a brilliant surgeon, and we don't want to lose you. Let me know about anything else odd and send me a copy of that letter you already got. And as for your partner, do you work in the same department and has he gotten anything from your mother?"

Steve shook his head no, but stopped. "I don't know. I could see him hiding something just to not upset me. That wedding reception was hard enough to deal with. We both work in surgery."

Steve didn't want to lie to HR, especially if they would keep his mother away or whatever they would do. But this wasn't good they were both in the same department. What would happen now? Would Ned be so irate he left Steve?

CHAPTER 12

Ned wasn't pleased. He wasn't happy with Steve's mother trying to get Steve in trouble or whatever her cockamamie idiotic plan was for that letter to Steve at the hospital. He was furious with her. What a piece of work. Now their relationship was known by HR so they had to be careful with post surgery stress relief. But that was fine since Steve hadn't felt up to it. All due to the pregnancy, caused by those hormones in the first place.

Ned smiled and waved to people he knew in the hallway. Pretending like nothing was wrong. They had gotten done with a meeting in HR. Steve found out about the letter on Ned's car the day after the wedding. He wasn't happy Ned kept it a secret from him. And Ned found out about the letter Steve had gotten, which he wasn't happy that Steve had kept a secret from him. Then HR wasn't too happy that they continued to date knowing they were violating a hospital policy. Just an all around miserable meeting.

Ned grabbed his stuff out of his locker and was glad he rode his bike today. He needed to ride off some stress and think.

He was also pissed, that everyone in the meeting, even Steve, assumed that Ned would be the one to get a different job. Yes Steve was a surgeon, yes he had more skill, yes he made more money and was harder to replace than Ned, but still. Ned was just in a terrible mood. He finally had gotten to the day shift and now he had to start at the bottom of the totem pole somewhere else.

Ned walked out to his bike thinking. He could get a job in another department, but he wasn't specialized for the OB surgery floor and they didn't have surgeries all the time there. Plus he didn't think there was even an opening. He could work on the cardiac floor, but again he needed more training. So Ned had to leave the hospital. He was pissed.

He put on his helmet, put his backpack on, and took off for home. There were a lot of other hospitals in the area. Specialized cardiac hospitals, cancer, surgical centers, plastic surgery, but he didn't care for any of that. He liked being a general surgical nurse as he got to assist with a wide variety of surgeries. Plus those cardiac surgeries lasted a long time. He didn't want to deal with that.

Ned pedaled harder and tried to pay attention to the traffic. He didn't want to get run over and killed just because he was mad at everything coming down at once. He took some deep breaths and tried to focus on the muscles pedaling, the wind against his face, the burn in his thighs. Anything to keep him from focusing on the shit show that was his life.

The only good thing he had to look forward to right now was Henry and David's wedding that weekend. Maybe they would have some ideas. But then again, he would not pester David for legal advice on his wedding day. And he wasn't sure they were even getting married, but that was the only conclusion he could come up with. Ned sighed again and kept on pedaling.

* * *

STEVE HAD NOTICED Ned's bad mood earlier this week. It was obvious what the cause was. That he had talked to HR. Now they knew about their dating and Ned had to find another job. He felt like crap but didn't know what else he could do. Especially when his own mother had mailed a letter to HR. It's not like they could pretend that didn't happen.

So Steve had tried to not upset Ned, tried to give him a massage which Ned turned down because Steve was pregnant, tried to make dinner which Steve stopped him because he was pregnant and so on. He was about ready to climb the walls with Ned's mood and him stopping Steve from doing anything. They needed to have a talk.

But right now was not the time. Maybe tonight after Henry and David's thing or tomorrow morning. Maybe he could make French Toast and get Ned to open up. He would not apologize, he didn't choose his mother, but he was sorry for how she had messed up their lives already. And they had only just gotten together! It was enough to make you bang your head against the car door.

"Are you feeling ok?"

Ned reached over from the driver's seat and squeezed Steve's thigh. Steve held his hand and looked over at Ned. The sun was coming through the windows, highlighting the blond streaks in Ned's hair. It was gorgeous. Steve was amazed again that Ned had never been a model. Ned had been approached though, but wasn't sure the people were from a legit agency. At least that's what Ned told him. He believed

Ned, but that still would be something to point to an ad and say 'that's my man'.

"I'm feeling fine. Just thinking of my mother and all her bullshit."

Ned squeezed his hand. They continued to hold hands and sit in comfortable silence as they drove to Henry and David's.

* * *

THERE WERE QUITE a few cars in the driveway and street. Steve wondered how many people were invited to this get together. He also wondered if Ned was right that it was a wedding in disguise. Steve half wished it wasn't, so he could ask Henry about his pregnancy and hold their baby. But then half of him wanted a nice wedding, one he could enjoy.

There was a sign on the door to go to the backyard, so they followed the arrow to the side, crossed the little Japanese wooden bridge, which was adorable, and into a rose garden. There were several people already in the backyard. He recognized Henry and David from their Facebook profiles. They were both in suits with David carrying the little baby.

He spotted Penny holding her arms out, trying to convince David to let her hold the baby.

"Hey, what is the name of their baby?" He glanced over at Ned who was smiling at the couple. Ned turned to look at Steve. He felt warmth and happiness looking at Ned. Steve was so content.

"I don't know. I don't think they had a name when I visited Henry in the hospital. I'm sure they have one now though." Ned grabbed Steve's hand, and they continued walking towards the couple holding hands.

Steve noticed a buffet set up along the back landscaping. There was even a portable bar set up with a bartender. Wow, this had to be a wedding. He was glad they wore slacks and not jeans or shorts like they had planned.

"Ned! Steve! I'm glad you could make it!" Henry gave them each a hug, but a longer one for Ned. He knew Ned had helped get them together, but he didn't know the whole story. Maybe he introduced them?

Penny came over for a hug too. "You look so happy and content. You're glowing too. Are you pregnant?"

Steve couldn't hide anything from Penny. He blushed and nodded his head. Penny yelled and gave him another tighter hug. He laughed as they rocked back and forth.

Ned put his arm around Steve's shoulders and looked at Henry and David, who had wandered over after Penny's scream.

"We've got something we'd like to share. Steve and I will be parents soon."

Steve was surrounded by people he didn't know. All were congratulating him, hugging and patting his stomach. He didn't like random people touching his belly, like being pregnant made him community property? He stepped half behind Ned and whispered in his ear that people kept rubbing his belly. Ned wrapped an arm around Steve's belly and one around his shoulders. That should keep them away, right? He hoped so.

Finally, it had cleared out and they could see David and the baby. He was itching to hold the baby. He didn't know what it was, he'd blame it on pregnancy hormones like anything else these days, but he was crazy for babies. David handed over the little bundle that was sleeping and Steve just stared at the little eyelashes, eyebrows, button nose, little lips. She was so cute.

Tears were welling in his eyes. He felt so much love for the baby growing inside of him. He had a piece of Ned inside him. It overwhelmed him sometimes.

"What is her name?"

"We named her Elizabeth Pat Bianchi, after Henry's parents."

That was so moving. And there goes the tears running down his face. He looked at Ned, but he was ready with a corner of the baby blanket, wiping away Steve's tears. Steve looked down at the little angel and sniffed her head. Such a clean, baby smell. He couldn't wait for their baby to arrive. He knew it would hurt coming out, but he was so ready for his own little angel.

"She is just the cutest thing ever."

"Thank you." David was near Steve, not crowding, but watching baby Elizabeth. Steve smiled and then handed the baby back, to ease David's concerns. He could even see the tension leave David as he held Elizabeth again.

Steve put a hand on his own belly and held it there. He knew Ned would be just like David, protective and wrapped around their baby's finger. He looked over at Ned and tried to keep his tears from welling over. Stupid hormones.

Ned reached out and grabbed Steve's hand without even looking. He loved that that they were so close they couldn't bear to be apart. He squeezed Ned's hand and smiled when Ned looked over.

"You two are the cutest couple I've seen. Besides David and I."

They all laughed. "Don't tell Penny that or it will get to her head."

They had all been helped out by Penny's amazing knack for bringing people together. She knew she was hot stuff, and didn't let David forget it, as she was his secretary.

"I wonder who she will pair up next?"

They all shrugged their shoulders. David leaned over to Henry and said something. Henry smiled and set his beer down on a rock lantern in the garden. The couple walked over to Penny and handed the baby to her. She was pleased to be holding little Elizabeth. Steve squeezed Ned's hand again. He couldn't wait for their baby.

"Attention everyone. Thanks for coming to our shindig. We had an ulterior motive." Henry grabbed David's hand and looked forward again. "We're getting married!"

Everyone cheered and clapped. Except for a loud "What?" which was quickly shushed by the big Italian looking guy. A minister walked off the deck at the back of the house to where the happy couple was standing. Ned was right, they were getting married right now. He felt full of love and happiness at that moment. He hoped he'd get his happy ever after too.

The group gathered around the couple as the minister performed the wedding ceremony. Penny held Elizabeth near the couple, but was back far enough to still be part of the crowd. As the couple kissed the crowd let out huge cheers. Except for one voice "I can't believe you didn't let me know! Your own mother!" Steve flinched and moved back. That was too close to what his mother was like. Ned put his arm around Steve's back and squeezed.

"That's David's mother. She loves him and would do nothing to hurt him. She goes overboard in loving and smothering him."

Steve nodded his head and watched the Italian woman, David's mother, squeeze his face with her hands and then give him a big sobbing hug. She did the same with Henry. And tried to do the same with Elizabeth but Penny wouldn't let her squeeze her cheeks. And then David's mom had her hands on her hips telling Penny that she was the grandmother and had more of a right to hold the grand baby than she did. Oh boy. Penny handed Elizabeth to David and stalked closer to David's mother. The look of terror on Henry and David's faces would have been comical if this wasn't their wedding. Henry jumped between the women and pushed Penny back. The Italian man, that must be David's father, pulled David's mother back. Hopefully they would keep to their respective corners of the backyard for the night.

"Wow. That was a close one. Now I know why David said he keeps Penny and his mother far apart."

Steve shook his head. He couldn't believe it was all over just like that. And people stood up to them and pulled them apart! It was a different world than what he was used to with his family. But a much better one.

"Time to toast the happy couple. Do you want anything other than a ginger ale?"

Steve hugged Ned and squeezed him tight. "Have I told you how much I love you?"

Ned kissed his cheek. "Yes. But I'll take it anytime you want to say it."

CHAPTER 13

*N*ed was getting ready for another surgery. He didn't enjoy coming to work anymore since Steve's mother had sent that letter. He still couldn't believe anyone could be so mean, let alone to their own child. He shook his head. Now they had a mess to deal with. He had to find a new job, away from Steve who was pregnant. He'd rather stay at the same hospital so he could check in on how Steve was doing, and just know that everything was ok. He cared for his omega, and he loved him.

But what were they going to do? People in the same department couldn't date. Since Ned would need more training to even apply for jobs in other departments, he would have to leave the hospital. And right after he got day shift too. He was not happy. Steve slammed his locker closed and then realized he was taking out his frustrations and instead needed to let it roll off of him. He paused and took a few deep breaths.

"Are you ok there?"

He opened his eyes to see Mike, another surgery team member.

"Yeah, just frustrated. Steve's mother is being... well, she alerted the hospital that Steve and I were dating. Now I have to find another job at another surgery place."

Mike's eyes grew wide. "You're kidding me!"

Ned shook his head. "I wish I was. She's a real piece of work."

Mike patted his shoulder. "Sucks. But why don't you get married? Then they can't do anything. You wouldn't be dating anymore."

Ned stared at Mike. Would it be that easy? Just get married?

"Are you sure? Getting married would get rid of the problem? We could both stay here?"

"Yes. That's what another surgery doc did when he was caught banging a nurse on the surgery team. They got married. They're both still here and have three kids together."

Ned felt like there was hope. He smacked Mike on the back. "Thank you so much for that idea. I think you might have just found a solution."

"Do it fast though. And don't tell them either. You could have a reception later."

Ned smiled and realized this sounded like a plan. He might run it by David just to make sure they weren't missing anything. Even though he only did family law, David was at least still a lawyer and could look over the hospital policy.

* * *

NED PARKED in his designated spot, grabbed the flowers he had bought for Steve and got out of his car. Things were looking up. He felt a lot better after talking to David today. But then again, maybe going to work somewhere else wasn't such a bad thing. He'd see what Steve had to say.

He walked in and called out "I'm home, Honey!". His smile was big as he imagined Steve's look when he saw the surprise he had brought. He bent down to look in the cabinets and reached back behind some stuff to grab the only vase they had. They combined their two households, and yet still only had one vase. He put the flowers in the vase, filled it with water and then walked back to find Steve.

Steve was in the bedroom laying on his side. He looked exhausted and pale. Flowers were forgotten.

"Steve! What's wrong?"

Steve limply waved a hand at him. "I'm fine. I'm just exhausted. I've been puking a lot. I thought it was supposed to stop?"

Ned put a hand to his forehead, it wasn't hot. He sat next to him and rubbed Steve's back. Ned felt guilty having all the fun and none of the hardship like Steve was.

"Is there anything I can do? Do you want some mint tea? Ginger ale? Soup?"

Steve shook his head. "No. I feel so tired. I'm just tired of this not feeling well."

Ned kept rubbing his back and worried. He knew some omegas could get sick due to the hormones. Everyone's body handled pregnancy different. Was there a problem with Steve's pregnancy?

"I wonder if you should get checked up tomorrow. I'm worried about how pale you are and so tired. That can't be good for the baby. Plus with you puking up food still, is the baby getting any nutrition?"

Steve laid there, staring at the lamp then he looked at Ned. "Yeah, maybe you're right."

Ned didn't want to scare himself, but he was alarmed at how Steve was acting. It was like he was drained with no energy. It was too late to meet with a doctor tonight, but maybe tomorrow they could get him in right away. As an emergency. Especially since he worked as a surgeon.

"Are you able to do surgery still?"

Steve nodded. "Yeah. I'm better in the morning. It's just the long day, being on my feet. I'm so tired."

Ned wondered. Was there such a thing as pregnancy anemia or something? He should get those baby books and read up on them. Steve had been devouring those books, and Ned had thought he didn't need to know anything since he wasn't the one going through the pregnancy. That shows what an ass he was. He was supposed to protect his omega, not let him fend for himself.

"I'll be right back. I'll heat some broth for you. Then I'll sit in here and read next to you, ok?"

Steve nodded his head and Ned left to make some chicken broth. The poor guy. He was still in his scrubs and had only taken off his shoes. Ned wondered if he could call anyone now to make sure they got in at 7 am. Or maybe they could just show up.

Ned heated the broth, put it on a tray and took it into the bedroom. He helped Steve sit up and fluffed pillows behind his back. The tray was on Steve's lap and he was drinking the broth. That's settled then. He went out into the living room searching for the baby books he knew Steve had. They were on the end table. Ned grabbed them along with the flowers. He hoped they didn't set off Steve's gag reflex. He was so touchy to smells.

"I got you some flowers to brighten up your day. Tiger lilies!" The smile on Steve's face was worth the cost. He set them on Steve's night table and gave him a quick kiss. Ned took off his clothes and then climbed in bed next to Steve. A nice night reading in bed. Nice, comfy and homey. He put his arm around Steve and hugged him.

"I love you, Honey. I'm so sorry this is wearing you down so bad. I wish I could take it away and bear it for you."

Steve kissed him on the cheek. "You've been wonderful."

Steve finished his broth and then snuggled back under the covers and laid down. "Can I help you get your scrubs off?"

"No. I want to lie down. I'll take them off later."

Ned was worried again that Steve was chilled. He felt his forehead, but Steve still wasn't hot.

He opened the first book <u>What to Expect When You're An Expecting Omega</u> and settled in to read about body changes and things to watch out for during pregnancy.

* * *

STEVE WALKED down the hallway to the doctor's door. He was glad that the doctor was able and willing to squeeze him into an early 7 AM appointment. If there was something that could be done for how he was feeling, he wanted it as soon as possible. Ned wanted to be at the appointment, but Steve was the one that said no. If it was something bad, he wanted to deal with it first, before having to deal with Ned's emotions too.

"Hi Dr. Andrews, thanks again for working me in." The doctor was a nice old man and had worked in OB/GYN for decades. One would think he was old fashioned or behind the times but he was the most progressive doctor in prenatal and maternity care at the hospital. He loved all the advances in science and care for patients.

"So, what seems to be the problem? You said you were tired?"

Steve sat down in a chair in front of Dr. Andrews desk. There was an exam room next door they could use if it was needed.

"I'm tired. Exhausted. I can make it through the day but collapse when I get home. I'm too tired to even take off my scrubs until I've laid down for a few hours. I'm pale too. And still nauseous and having a hard time keeping things down."

Dr. Andrews frowned. "I think we'll start off by doing blood tests. There may be a few things that could be resolved quickly. Have you noticed if you're bruising easy?"

Steve shook his head. "I haven't noticed it. The only symptoms I have are those I described."

Dr. Andrews nodded and wrote something on a pad on his desk. Then he looked up. "I've got a form here for some blood tests. I will do a quick exam now, to see how your skin reacts, your eyes... you know the drill."

Steve would have nodded, but he was too tired already. He was getting tired faster and faster as the days went on. Please don't let it be cancer. He was hoping for some anemia at the worst. That was easily treatable and not so bad to have.

Dr. Andrews pushed on his skin, checked his tongue, eyes and did various other non-invasive tests. Everything seemed to be fine, at least from what Steve could tell. He had done these same tests on himself last night in the bathroom. It was good to have a second opinion though.

"How are you handling being up and doing surgery for hours?"

Here was the question he had been dreading. He didn't want to admit it to himself, but last night he realized he had to. It involved his health, the health of the baby and the health of his patients.

"Not well. I'm exhausted. I've been sitting down during surgeries but I can't do that anymore. There are surgeries I can, but others I can't. I'm just too wiped out. I could lie down right now and sleep for a week or more."

Dr. Andrews flattened his lips and nodded. "I will put you on bed rest. I know it's not what you wanted to hear, but this pregnancy is draining you and you're not any good to anyone when you're like this. I'm being harsh here because I know you'd go right out there and do your job anyway ignoring my warnings, right?"

Steve had to smile. Dr. Andrews knew doctors well. Especially omegas with their need to take care and not let anyone down. "You're right."

"I know." He smiled to take the sting out of his words. "I'll submit paperwork for a bed rest for a week. Go down to the labs and get those tests done and then go home. Did you ride in with Ned? I suggest he drive you home, you're too tired, I can tell."

Steve blinked. "How did you know about Ned? I thought we were doing a good job of keeping it quiet?"

"Rumors fly fast around here. Especially when it's two people on the same floor. Has HR gotten ahold of you yet?"

Steve frowned. He wasn't happy that their secret, seemed to be common knowledge. "Yes. They want Ned to find another job and leave. We're not happy and are considering several ideas."

Dr. Andrews sat back down. "Yes, I can see that would not be ideal. Especially when you'd rather be close to your alpha instead of farther away. I suppose you know you can't <u>date</u> in the same department, right?"

Steve frowned. Wasn't that what they were just talking about? Dr. Andrews wasn't stupid, and he knew Steve wasn't either. What was he getting at? Damn he wished he wasn't so tired. He'd be able to pick this up better if he could think better.

"Yes, we can't date. But... what if we were married?" At that Dr. Andrews smiled. Gotcha. Looks like that idea may be the winner then. And it would keep both Ned and him close together, not far apart.

"I wonder if there's anything we have to do other than show up one day with a marriage certificate?"

"Oh I couldn't say anything about that, I don't know how HR works. But I think having things in writing and formalized would do a lot from a legal point of view."

Steve smiled and felt better than he had in days. Dr. Andrews was a life saver. "I have another question related to the baby. It's about... diseases that could be passed down."

Dr. Andrews frowned. "Have you had any genetic testing done that showed a concern?"

Steve shook his head. "No. It's my mother. Her behavior is bizarre. I'm worried that if she has a mental illness of some sort, that it will get passed down to my child."

Dr. Andrews nodded his head. "That's a good question and something to consider. However, If your mother hasn't been diagnosed and you and Ned haven't done genetic testing, there's no concrete advice I can give. There are odds for everything. You could have the genes for a disease but the environment also plays a big role in the disease manifesting. So I wouldn't worry."

Steve flattened his lips. That didn't do much to ease his concern.

"I realize you're worried, and it's natural for an expectant parent to worry. There's a good possibility that your mother's behavior may not be caused by a mental illness. And if it turns out it she has a personality disorder, and your child also has it, you'll be aware of the possibility. You can catch it early and get your child connected with the right people for treatment, medication and whatever is needed."

Steve nodded his head. That was true. "Thank you very much for squeezing me in again."

"No problem. I always felt you were one of our top surgeons and I hate to see anyone suffer, especially with their first pregnancy. Get those tests done so I can get the labs back. Have a good day and go right home young man!"

Steve laughed and stood up. He shook the doctor's hand and walked out of the office feeling so much better than when he had first walked in. Things were looking up.

CHAPTER 14

He walked onto the floor frowning. He couldn't help it, he was worried. Ned had driven them to work that morning, earlier than usual so Steve could make his appointment. He heard nothing much about it as he drove Steve home, other than it went well and some lab tests were ordered. Ned would like to have known which ones, but Steve was already out like a light. He was anxious about him. Ned wished he had some rights to ask Dr. Andrews what he thought and what the lab results were, but he knew as just a boyfriend, he had no rights to any of that.

This getting married idea was sounding better and better. His parents would be surprised, but they'd be fine with a fast wedding. Steve's parents, he wondered if they could get by without inviting them. He didn't want a three ring circus, especially with a nasty woman like Steve's mother. He shuddered just thinking about what she would say at their wedding. They were not inviting Steve's parents.

Ned took the elevator down to the cafeteria and got in line. He missed Steve already. He was glad Steve was on bed rest though. That guy worked himself too hard, but that just shows what a good doctor he was.

"Hey, Ned!" Ned felt a tap on his arm and turned around.

"I'm Mike in pharmacy. Dr. Andrews told me to run you down. There's something to pick up in the pharmacy if you want to run them home to Dr. Wilder."

Ned's eyebrows rose. Wow. Then he got nervous. Is it bad if the pharmacists chases you down? Oh, God. His stomach dropped. He got out of line and walked as fast as he could to the elevators. He waited about 10 seconds and then decided running down the stairs might be faster. Should he call Dr. Andrews? No, that would bother the doctor. He would find out everything at the pharmacy. Ned could wait, it might not be bad news. Maybe Dr. Andrews just wanted Steve to get relief or whatever quickly?

He looked up at the elevator sign, but both were stuck on other floors. Ned knew trying to get to the pharmacy from here would take longer than just waiting for the elevator. But it was killing him. He chewed on his thumb. Ned hadn't done that since, he couldn't remember. He knew it was a bad habit in middle school. He took years to break that habit. It involved all the nasty tasting goop on the ends of his fingers to break him of it. And now he had just started up again.

Oh thank God the elevator was here. He somewhat patiently waited for everyone to get off, he wasn't a heathen, and then got on the elevator. He felt like an idiot just going down a floor, but he knew the layout of the hospital and it was a pain to use the stairs. The stairs were in the corners, and everything you wanted to go to was near the middle, where the elevators were.

The doors opened so slowly Ned was tempted to push them open faster. He couldn't believe how calm everyone else was. His world could collapse, Steve could have some disease and everyone was wandering around like no big deal. He squeezed between the doors and jogged to the pharmacy. Ned didn't care if he got odd looks, his omega needed him.

"Hi." He was not stopping to catch his breath. He was not breathing hard. Nope. He wasn't out of shape. "I'm here for Dr. Wilder's prescriptions?"

The pharmacist looked in the computer and grabbed a large bag. Why did he have a large bag? What was wrong with Steve?

"Are you allowed to collect pharmacy items for the patient?"

Ned blinked. "I think so. We live together. I'm picking them up for him. He's home on bed rest."

"I see nothing here in the computer. I'll need his authorization." Oh, you've got to be kidding me. "He needs to sign this form and then we can release them to you."

Ned wanted to reach out and shake the pharmacy tech something fierce. He counted to three, all the while staring at the poor tech like he was an imbecile. "I need the meds now. How can I get a signed form if he's home on bed rest, probably asleep. I can try calling him? Would that work?"

"I'll check but I'm not sure." The tech left and Ned ran his hands through his hair. He would seriously force choke this day. He couldn't pick up meds for his omega? Who was pregnant with his baby? This was so ridiculous he didn't know of a word strong enough for what this was.

"That will not work. We need a signed authorization."

Ned felt brain cells crawling out of his ears. Anytime he went against the stupidity of bureaucracy, he lost brain cells. He swore he did. It was a miracle he had any left.

"I'm on lunch break. I can't drive home, wake him up, get him to sign something, then drive back, get the meds, drive home, then drive back here. Can I FaceTime him? Skype him? Something that shows it's him?"

The tech shook his head. "Sorry. We ensure the privacy of our patients and their medical needs. I'm sorry but we need to have a signed release."

Ned sighed and looked up at the ceiling. He couldn't do it. He couldn't make it home and back and do all this running around before he had to be back at work. Ned didn't want to take an emergency PTO and have someone cover for him. What could he do?

"Is there any authorization in the hospital paperwork that shows Dr. Wilder allows me be privy to his medical info? You know, when you register to get admitted, one question is who they can share the info with. Is that in the hospital database? I need to get these meds to him."

Ned was hoping that he hadn't just whined that last part, but he might have. He wasn't above begging or pleading right now.

The tech pursed his lips and looked at Ned.

"Please? He's home sick. He went to the doctor this morning and was put on bed rest. We were waiting for the lab test results. I've been working all morning. He didn't answer when I called to check on him. I'm sure he's sleeping, but he probably needs these meds."

"Let me see what I can do." The tech left again. Ned rubbed his eyes. Why? Why was this happening? All of a sudden, things were popping up determined to screw up their lives. Ned pulled out his phone and decided it couldn't hurt to get Steve on FaceTime or something. The phone rang and rang.

"Hello?"

Ned sighed with relief. "Hi Honey. How are you doing?"

"I'm so tired. I can't stay awake." Steve sounded half asleep.

"Did you eat anything for lunch?"

"No, you woke me up."

Ned chewed his thumb again and wondered if he could call someone to feed Steve. Maybe he could get a reduced work schedule or something so he could have a longer lunch period to go home and make sure Steve ate over lunch? Was he even drinking enough liquids?

"Have you drank anything since you got home?"

"I went right to bed. I have water here." Ned shook his head. Steve needed someone to take care of him right now. Who was available that could run errands? Think, think.

"Hi, I'm the pharmacist. You had some questions?"

"Hold on, Honey. Yeah, I'm here to pick up the meds for Dr. Wilder. He's at home on bed rest for a week. He came in this morning for lab tests but needs those meds. Isn't there any way I can get them and take them home to him?" This was ridiculous.

"We would need a signed release form. He's got a flag that no one other than him can have any medical information regarding him." Probably because of his nosy, crazy mother. Damn her.

"Honey, I can't pick up your meds for you because there's no release allowing me. Can you turn on FaceTime or sign something and fax it in? Then I could get these home to you."

"Yeah." Ned looked at the phone and then Steve's face appeared. He was so pale. Ned's heart clenched. He turned the phone around and handed it to the pharmacist. Ned felt vindicated when the pharmacist's eyebrows rose.

"Hello doctor. Does--" A quick glance to his name tag. "Ned Patterson have permission to pick up your prescriptions?"

"Yes. All the time. Put him on my list of people allowed to discuss my medical information."

"Ok, that's all we needed." Ned took the phone back.

"I'm so sorry to bother you like this. Go back to sleep and I should be there in 30 minutes with the meds."

Steve nodded his head and turned the phone off. It looked like he had fallen asleep again. Ned prayed it was nothing that couldn't be easily cured.

SEVERAL DAYS LATER, Steve was amazed how much better he felt. How amazing modern medicine was, just a quick shot to the butt, and he felt better. The bed rest was nice too. The daily B12 pills helped as well. Now Ned could stop freaking out. Steve shook his head remembering how freaked out Ned had been after driving like the wind to get home with his meds. Just B12 anemia, nothing that a shot and pills couldn't take care of. Everything was going fine now.

He was lounging in his robe on the couch in the living room watching whatever on Netflix. Some odd show about some kids on bikes. He had his suit all laid out on the bed, but didn't want to put it on until Ned showed up. He wanted no wrinkles on it. Or food. Now he was feeling so much better, his appetite had come back too. He felt like he was constantly eating. Right now it was apples with peanut butter. Yum, yum, yum.

The door opened, he looked over to see Ned walk in with a huge smile on his face.

"Are you nervous?" Steve laughed. He was more excited than nervous. What a reason to have a rushed marriage.

"Do you think we can tell everyone it was a shotgun wedding?" Ned laughed and leaned over to kiss him.

"Come on, get up and get your suit on Honey. It's time to make an honest man out of you." Steve couldn't stop smiling either. They were getting married at the courthouse. It was a quick, small and private wedding. They were doing it fast so that neither one had to get a different job, but also because the shenanigans involved in getting Steve's meds had opened their eyes to what a nightmare it might be if they weren't married and anything else happened.

Steve waddled to the bedroom and shut the door. No peeking before the wedding. He knew it was silly of him to close the door, but he felt like a gigantic waddling duck. Steve hadn't wanted Ned to touch him since he started showing. He had used a mirror several times to see stretch marks growing on his once flat abs. What would Ned think?

He pulled on his gray pin striped suit with a light gray shirt. A light blue tie with thin gray stripes. Then the suit jacket. Ned had to buy a maternity suit that had the top of the suit pants made just like regular maternity pants. At least none of his suits had to get cut up to fit him. Which had been Plan B if Ned couldn't find a maternity suit in the right size.

Steve walked out into the living room. Ned's smile grew so big that it looked like there wasn't any more room on his face to smile another millimeter bigger.

"So how do I look?" He was self conscious about being big. He knew Ned loved him the way he was, but Ned kept himself fit bicycling and lifting weights. Steve had done nothing but lie around lately.

"You look beautiful. As always. But especially today." Steve felt the tears welling up in his eyes. He closed his eyes trying not to cry. Steve didn't want to get all blotchy and be a red mess for the photos. He assumed there would be photos.

"Will there be photos?" He opened his eyes and looked at Ned. He left all the details up to Ned as he wanted to rest and not get stressed out.

"Yes. I think our friends will take tons of photos." Steve nodded his head. He was a little sad that they weren't having an extravagant wedding, but he knew it would have been impossible to keep that a secret. And the reason they needed to keep it a secret? His mother. His ever so delightful mother ruining anything she got her hands on.

"I'm sorry my mother ruins everything." Ned looked surprised. He wrapped Steve in a hug and just held him. "Steve, I don't care about your mother, I care about you. If this isn't a wedding you want, let me know and I'll change it. I want you to be happy."

Steve teared up even more now, just when he thought he might have gotten his tears under control. He was so lucky to have Ned as his alpha. He knew no one else that would be so supportive and willing to put up with a mother-in-law from hell.

"Don't sell yourself short. It's not your fault you have a fruit-cake mother. I will do whatever it takes to keep you happy and our wedding as stress free as possible."

Steve raised his head and looked at Ned. He was so hand-some in his dark gray suit. He looked magnificent. So hot. If he felt any better, he would have insisted on a little action before the ceremony. He was that hot. But they had a dead-line. They were slotted for 2 PM.

"I love you. This is perfect. Just close friends. We've made our own family."

* * *

Their wedding would be held in the courthouse at the Clerk of Courts office. As informal as possible. That's what Steve preferred. He wasn't sure what Ned wished as he did whatever Steve wanted regarding the wedding. Steve guessed it didn't matter the size of the wedding in the long run, they would be married and that's all that mattered.

He was nervous and Little Bub had been pressing on his bladder. Steve already had to the hit the bathroom right when they got to the courthouse. Hopefully he'd make it through the wedding with no need to run to the bathroom.

He looked over at Ned. They had their corsages on that matched. Henry and David were there with little Elizabeth, Penny, and Ned's parents. They invited no one else, because it was last minute and their friends couldn't get time off at such a late notice. But that was ok. They would have a reception at Ned's parent's house at a later date. Right after the wedding, they were going to a restaurant. Ned's parents were the perfect parents. Thrilled for them both, excited to be grandparents and let the kids, who were adults, live their own lives.

The judge entered the room in his robes. Which they had asked if it was possible for the judge to wear his robes. Those black robes were cool and lent an air of formality to the proceedings. About the only level of formality there, other than everyone in suits or dresses. Penny outshone everyone in her silver and white 50s style dress with white gloves. She was stunning.

Ned grabbed his hand. "Are you ready?" Steve nodded and smiled. He had butterflies, and he was sure Little Bub had butterflies too. But since those B12 shots and pills he had been feeling tons better. He didn't have to worry about fainting or puking. Thank God.

They walked up to the judge. He said a few words, and then they were pronounced married. Steve hoped someone took a pic of Ned's smirk during the questions. He looked so handsome. They leaned over and kissed to applause and cheers. Even Elizabeth gave a cute little yowl.

They signed the marriage license, their witnesses signed, and it was done. Steve felt such relief. He hadn't realized he was so tense that his mother might show up to ruin things. It didn't matter now, they were married! They picked out matching plain gold bands. Simple, yet gorgeous.

"We are so glad Ned found you." Ned's mother gave Steve a hug. It was amazing to have a mother take to him and be proud. He felt tears forming. She pulled back and then Ned's dad stepped in to give him a hug. He was struck speechless. Tears were now rolling out of his eyes.

"You are just perfect. I'm glad to call you my son." And there went his composure.

"Thank you. I'll help Steve freshen up and then we'll meet you at the restaurant. It's just a few blocks away. It's called Minerva's."

* * *

NED OPENED every door for him and gave him a kiss when Steve walked through them. It was adorable until about the third door. He wanted to get to the bathroom as quickly as possible. It was odd kissing your new husband as he holds the door open to the bathroom.

They made their way out the front door with their small group. Steve was too wrapped up trying to walk down the courthouse steps without falling to notice anything. His belly was so big he had faith he had feet, but he sure couldn't see them.

"Look at that woman. She looks unbalanced."

Ned would go down one step, wait and hold Steve's hand to help him down the step. It was a pain as there was no guardrail but Ned worked out pretty well. He was just worried Ned would fall backwards down the steps.

"She's coming this way. Does she know any of us?"

It was slow going down all these steps. Why did the courthouse have so many steps? If he wanted a workout, he'd go to the gym.

"You have shamed this family for the last time! I thought you would come to your senses and appreciate your family--"

Steve looked up as the yelling woman registered in his mind. It was his mother. Of course it was. He didn't understand how she had found out about his wedding, but there she was. Embarrassing him and making a spectacle of herself.

"--but you have done everything possible to embarrass me. I won't stand it! You need to cooperate! I didn't raise you to act this way!"

He could only stand there and stare. He was pregnant and all his mother could think about was herself. Steve didn't know why he continued to be surprised at the level of narcissism she showed. It was if she was in a contest with herself to top whatever she had done before.

"Hey lady, you need to back up and go away. You're harassing and I can call the police."

He recognized David's voice, but he couldn't look. Steve could only stare at his mother's angry face, pinched into a furious face directed at him. What did he ever do to deserve this?

Steve's staring was interrupted by Ned's face appearing in front of him. "Come on Honey, move with me. We need to turn around. I need you to move. Can you move for me? Steve?"

He came out of it and let Ned turn him around to walk back up the steps. Steve heard David trying to contain his mother. Penny was already at the top of the steps getting a security guard. He was so embarrassed.

"No Honey, don't cry. Don't cry. This day is perfect. We got married. Believe nothing she said."

Steve knew what she was saying wasn't true, but it was hard not to let it affect him. He was pregnant and had just gotten married. Emotions were running high right now.

Ned opened the door to the courthouse and pulled Steve in. Steve looked back through the glass door to see security guards holding his mother. A police car pulled up. She kicked a guard. Swung her purse at another one. The police ran up the steps. She was handcuffed now. It took both of the policemen to get her down the steps to the car. No, that wasn't working anymore. She was fighting somehow and not going any closer to the cop car.

"Honey, are you sure you want to watch this? It's upsetting."

Steve looked at Ned. He wondered if he was in shock. "It all seems so surreal. She's never been this bad before."

Ned wrapped his arms around Steve and held him. As much as Ned could with Steve's big belly. "I'm so sorry. But you're not the person she says you are. You are perfect. I love you. Don't forget that." Steve nodded his head.

The front door opened again. Ned released him from the hug. David and Penny were back inside.

"Are you ok, Steve?" He nodded. "Yeah. I didn't think she'd show up today. I don't know how she found out."

David shook his head.

"Oh, Steve." Penny gave him a big hug and patted his head.

"I dealt with the police. I suggested a psych hold. She was acting crazy enough for it. This way she'll get evaluation and get on medication if she needs it."

Penny stepped back. Ned wrapped an arm around Steve's waist. Henry was next to David now with little Elizabeth.

"I think it's the best for her. She's gotten worse over the years, but she hit a new low with her craziness these last few months." Ned rubbed his back. Steve leaned against Ned.

"Well, let's go to our wedding reception at the restaurant. I could use a drink." Ned smiled and winked at Steve. Only Ned could brush this off so easily and get Steve focusing on the positive. He was so glad he had married Ned.

"I love you, Ned." He smiled. "I know."

They kissed to the groans and laughter of their friends.

CHAPTER 15

"Oh look, you can see its feet!" Ned leaned in closer to make out other features of the baby on the ultrasound monitor. Nothing smacked you upside the head you were having a baby like watching the ultrasound. And listening to the heart beat. When the technician turned up the audio so that the strong heartbeat was blasted out the speakers, Ned had to sit down and put his head down so he wouldn't faint. It was odd, he knew before that moment he was a dad, but seeing the baby and hearing the heartbeat just solidified it into reality.

Steve laughed until the tech asked him to stop as it was affecting the ultrasound. "Have pity on me, I got a huge shock." Ned was playing for sympathy here.

"What, you didn't realize I was pregnant until now? Did you think this was due to too many beers after work or something?" Ned smirked and looked up.

"Actually.... I do think it was due to too many beers. But during the day. After the wedding reception." Now it was

Ned's turn to chuckle as Steve blushed and looked at the tech. Ned didn't care, he was sure the tech knew how babies were made. It was cute that Steve was still somewhat embarrassed about it.

"I can't believe it's getting closer. Soon he'll be here. Or she. Do you want to know the gender?" Steve looked at Ned, but he wasn't sure what he wanted. Ned wanted it to be a surprise, and yet he wanted to know immediately.

"What do you want, Honey?" He would leave it up to Steve. He was the one carrying the baby. Either way, there would be little doctor scrubs and stethoscopes in that child's future. You could bet on it.

"I'd like to wait. Let it be a surprise." Ned smiled and squeezed Steve's hand. It would be a surprise then. Something to look forward to after the long wait for the pregnancy to be over.

* * *

THE TIME WENT BY QUICKLY. Steve was back at work assisting on surgeries while sitting down, if he could help over his big belly. He hated waddling down the hallway at work. Ned thought it was adorable, but Ned's sense of humor did not translate well to a pregnant Steve. Like the ducky umbrella Ned had bought him. Because Steve waddled. Ned thought it was adorable. Steve chased him around the apartment screaming and trying to beat him over the head with it.

Ned was doing a great job of taking care of his omega. Rubbing his feet. Putting on compression socks so that Steve's ankles wouldn't swell up so bad it hurt. Propping him up in bed or in the rocker so he could sleep sitting up. The heartburn was an absolute pain during the last few months.

Steve thought his throat was getting eaten through by all the heartburn. Everything set it off.

The poor guy was miserable and Steve couldn't even take a bath to relax because he couldn't fit in their tub anymore. The night Steve found that out, was the night Ned had to deal with a sobbing mess of a pregnant man. He ordered an Uber just to get the guy to pick up ice cream and flowers and deliver it. It was probably the most expensive Uber ride ever, but Ned didn't care. Anything was worth it to make Steve feel better.

Steve being miserable with painful ankles, back pain, heartburn, stretch marks galore and not sleeping well was taking its toll on Ned. He couldn't believe the last few weeks were hell with such sleep deprivation and then they were supposed to take care of a newborn baby needing constant around the clock care? Ned wanted to ask Henry how they had handled it, but he didn't want to look like he wasn't a good alpha. He hoped his parents and friends would help out. Penny. She was the one who set them up on the blind date after all. So this was all her fault. He'd remind her of that when they needed a break.

* * *

NED HADN'T WANTED to work this week because Steve was getting fake contractions, the Braxton-Hicks contractions. Why did the body have to fake contractions? The body was still a mystery why it did things, even in this day and age. Steve was so miserable that Ned felt guilty about his joy over getting to escape and go to work. If that baby didn't come soon, Ned would be bald from pulling out his hair. Pregnancy was hard.

Ned was looking over his prep notes when his phone vibrated. He looked at the screen and saw it was Steve. He sighed. He wondered what it was this time. Ice cream? Sugar scrub with lavender oil to make his stretch marks go away? He was tempted to not answer it, but knew that was selfish. Plus, with it this late in the pregnancy, it would be stupid to miss a call.

"Hi Honey, how are you doing?"

"It's here. I mean its timing. I mean it's time! It's coming! My water broke!" Ned dropped the folder and looked around trying to remember what they were supposed to do. Oh right, get to the hospital.

"Ok, calm down. Everything will be fine. We need to get to the hospital now. I'll go put your go bag in the car and then drive you in. Just hang on and calm down."

"Honey, you're at the hospital right now." Ned smiled and rubbed his forehead.

"I know. But you're not driving yourself in here. And we don't need an ambulance."

"It's in the afternoon. There will be traffic. I don't want to wait. What if it pops out while we're on the interstate? I don't want to be on TV with my legs spread wide on the side of the road!" Ned bit his lips to keep from laughing. The image in his head was ridiculous.

"Well I'm not leaving you to have some stranger drive you here. I'm driving you here. Remember what they said in Lamaze class? The first baby takes the longest. It will be hours yet. No big deal -- "

"No. Big. Deal?" Ned knew he had just screwed up. Big time.

"I'm sorry I didn't mean that. This is a huge deal--"

"You're damn right it is! This is a very big deal. A baby the size of a bowling ball is coming out something the size of a pea! This is an enormous deal!"

Ned wasn't sure how he would get Steve calmed down. High blood pressure was a danger in the later stages of pregnancy. Especially during delivery and the weeks after. The maternity mortality rate in the United States was the absolute worst for First World countries. Ned had vowed Steve would not be one of those statistics.

"Honey, I'm worried about your blood pressure. Remember? We need to keep you calm so you don't get Pre-Eclampsia. Can you do some deep breathing with me?" Ned wondered if there was anyone he could call to help keep Steve calm until he got there.

"Ok, ok, yeah that's a good idea. I'll do some deep breaths now." Ned heard Steve taking several slow deep breaths. That was good.

"Now go sit in your rocking chair, or lie down on the bed. I'll call someone to come over and be with you. Would that be ok?" He knew better than to order Steve around right now. That was now one of Steve's pet peeves these last few weeks as he got crabbier and crabbier. But he was not going to tell Steve that.

"No. I want no one here, it will make me more nervous. Just get here. I'll go lay down."

"Ok. Put me on speakerphone so you can tell me when you've laid down in bed. I'll get my stuff and tell them I'm leaving." Ned grabbed his stuff out of his locker, poked his head into the floor director's office and told him the baby was coming right now.

"Congratulations! And good luck!" Ned waved and jogged to the stairs. He was too eager to wait for the elevators. He needed to move or explode. He was so excited and terrified at the same time. It was an odd feeling.

* * *

NED DROVE SO CAREFULLY to the hospital, Steve was about ready to push him out the door and drive himself. But he calmed himself down by breathing deep and reminding himself of what a careful, good driver Ned was. And how much Ned cared about them to drive like that. That lasted about one mile.

"Can you step on it, Honey? Or you will be seeing me giving birth on the side of the road on TV tonight."

Ned scowled and punched the gas to jump up to 24 miles an hour. Oh yeehaw. They'd make it to the hospital by the time their kid hit his third birthday.

"Honey. I'm in labor. I'm having pains here. Can you at least drive the speed limit?"

"I don't want to get in a wreck! You can get in a wreck if you drive too fast." Steve looked over at Ned and just stared. He doubted Ned had ever driven slow in his life before today. It was adorable how concerned Ned was, but Steve didn't feel like anything was adorable at the moment. His back hurt, the cramping was killing him and more stuff was running down his legs. He wanted this over with. Could he request a c-section? Was that a thing?

"Do you think I could request a c-section? I'm not looking forward to pushing and spending hours with these contractions. It hurts worse than the time I ate 12 tacos in one sitting. I'm dying here."

"Honey, I'm going as fast as I can." Ned was still staring at the road with wide eyes and white knuckles on the steering wheel. Steve was sure that if he yelled boo Ned would go through the roof. He looked at the side window and concentrated on breathing deep and feeling the baby.

Was there a heartbeat? Was there movement? Hell if he knew. Everything seemed right and his last checkup was perfect. Everything would be fine today. It was funny that he was the worrier, but now Ned was freaking out and Steve was the calm one. Steve smiled and wondered what their baby would look like. Black hair or brown? Blue eyes or brown? Who would the baby look like?

* * *

STEVE WALKED another loop around the delivery room with Ned helping. Steve couldn't sit or lay through the pain. He had to get up and move. He didn't know how anyone managed to just lie there through the pain. Ned looked like he had gone a week without sleep in the middle of a war. Poor guy was stressed out. Steve put his hand on Ned's arm and tried to send calming thoughts his way. He didn't think it worked, but at least one of them wasn't freaking out.

Steve stopped and breathed quick and shallow just like he learned in Lamaze classes. The contractions were coming fast and close now. Finally, after 10 hours maybe they were near done. It was 2 in the morning and he was tired of this.

"Honey, why don't we get you in the bed. The nurse wants to check how far you're dilated again. And it will give you a rest. I don't think you can walk anymore. These contractions are coming too close now."

Steve could only nod his head. He was having trouble staying upright now. Ned and a nurse half carried him to the bed and got him back on the mattress. Ned wiped his forehead and kissed his skin.

"You're doing great Honey. I'm so proud of you. In a little bit our baby will be here."

"Great. Go pick it up at Target. I don't want to do this anymore."

Steve squeezed Ned's hand and kept doing his shallow breathing. Finally, the hours of pain would be over.

"Ok, now push." The doctor was at the end of the bed ready to catch. Steve closed his eyes and pushed and pushed. It felt like something might have moved. He heard a crying baby and his entire body melted into the mattress. Tears rolled down his face. They had done it! Their baby was here and healthy.

"I love you Honey. You were amazing." Ned kissed his cheek and kept holding Steve's hand while they wiped the baby off and tied off the umbilical cord.

The nurse came over with their little wrapped up bundle. "Congratulations you two. You have a baby girl!"

Steve and Ned looked at each other. A girl? They had never talked about it, but they had both been expecting a boy!

"Do you have a name picked out for a girl?" Ned shook his head no still looking shell shocked. "I thought for sure it would be a boy. Do you?"

Steve gave a soft chuckle while he looked down at their baby's perfect face. Black hair and blue eyes. Just like him. He knew the hair could lighten and the eyes could turn brown, but for now the girl looked just like him. It was such an amazing miracle to hold something he had made and knew so well over the last several months.

"I thought of the name Penelope Ophelia Patterson." Ned hugged them both and kissed both their cheeks.

"It's a beautiful name. Did you realize the initials spell out POP though?"

Steve looked over at Ned with a slack face. "Oh, no. I was set on that name!"

Ned laughed and gave him a quick kiss. "That's ok Honey. She's our little pop of joy!"

CHAPTER 16

At home, Ned held Penelope against his chest as he burped her. Steve scooted back down in the bed and closed his eyes. This eating every few hours was wearing them both out. But they wouldn't change it for the world. Ned looked down at Penelope and smiled. He couldn't believe he was a dad. Sure, the evidence was right in front of him, literally in his arms. But it was still a shock.

He moved his head a little to sniff in that new baby smell. Ned had always thought women were nuts mentioning how they loved that new baby smell. Like it was a new car or something. He felt he should now apologize to all the mothers out there. They weren't kidding, there really was a new baby smell. Ned couldn't get over how soft her hair was, how smooth her skin, how tiny her fingers were. She was a little miracle. And to think they had made her.

A loud snuffing noise broke the quiet. Ned held the baby closer and tried to not giggle. His chest was shaking. He would wake Penny up if he kept this up. But it was no use.

Steve's snores were hilarious. They weren't your typical snore sound.

Steve looked so peaceful in sleep. They both had dark circles under their eyes. The lack of sleep wasn't that hard to deal with. They were used to not having enough sleep in their profession. Especially with Steve's profession as a doctor.

Ned carefully scooted off the bed. He walked around to Steve's side and put Penny in her crib. Steve didn't want their baby in another room away from them. He had said it was just wrong to have someone be so close to you for months and then far away. If it helped Steve and Penny sleep through the night better, then Ned was all for it. And from what he'd heard, Penny was sleeping a lot longer than other babies had at her age. Having Penny and Steve near each other was probably the cause. Ned leaned over and kissed Penny's forehead. He walked back around and got into bed. Ned turned off his lamp and scooted close to Steve.

* * *

"I DON'T KNOW. I don't think we should take her out this soon."

Ned stared at Steve. He knew Steve was just being a protective parent which Ned loved, but Ned really wanted all of them to be outside on a blanket in the park. Enjoying the weather. They didn't even have to do anything. Just sit there, hold Penny, watch everyone and enjoy the day.

"Honey, I want to show off my family. If we took her in an enclosed place, like the mall where fresh air isn't circulating then I'd agree with you. But we're going to the park."

Steve didn't look convinced. He was holding Penny like Ned would take her away. Ned sighed.

"What if we went to Henry and David's? Sat in their backyard?"

"They have all those flowers. There's bees." Ned blinked. He wondered if all new omega parents were like this, or if Steve was showing signs of crazy. Ned thought about it. If Steve had his mother's issues, he would have shown it a long time ago. Especially with a high stress job of being a doctor. He could only assume this was new omega parentitis.

"Ok. Maybe just a week old is too soon. Let's pretend we're outside. I'll make sandwiches, we can sit on a blanket and watch a nature documentary in the living room. How does that sound?"

Steve nodded his head and relaxed his arms around Penny. "Why do you want to go outside so bad?"

Ned smiled. "Because we've been cooped up in here over a week with nothing but feed the baby, change the baby, sleep. I'm dying for a change of routine. Plus I like being outside."

"I haven't even thought of that. I feel like I'm just surviving. I'm still so short on sleep."

Ned could tell. Steve was still dragging. Even with the B12. They were both dragging. The only one doing well was Penny, and that was what parent's did. They sacrificed for their children. Maybe Ned could buy some new bed sheets. Some new change in the place where they spent all their time now. Steve looked content on the couch.

"What if I got us some new bed sheets? Something new in the bedroom so it doesn't look the same as it has been all week. I'm just dying to get out."

Steve narrowed his eyes. "The last time you had to get out, you came back with that duck umbrella."

Ned snorted and covered his mouth trying to make himself stop giggling. That umbrella fiasco was hysterical.

"Maybe I'll come back with duck sheets and a ducky comforter? You never know."

"If you bring anything back relating to my waddling, you'll be sleeping out in the living room." Ned smiled. Steve was so much fun to tease.

"You're not waddling anymore, Honey."

"I feel as big as an elephant still. I thought I'd get my body back the second I gave birth."

Ned's eyebrows lifted. "Didn't you read all those parenting books? Didn't they say anything about that?"

Steve shook his head. "I only read about body changes before giving birth and the labor and delivery parts. I don't even know if they cover the body after giving birth."

Ned looked at Steve and tried to think of what would help him out right now. What would make him feel better?

"What about a bath? Should I get Epsom salts and you could take a bath? You haven't been able to take one in months."

Steve's eyes lit up. "I would love that. Could you get scented Epsom salts?"

* * *

STEVE TOOK another deep breath and relaxed. The water was hot. Lavender scent filled the bathroom. He missed taking hot baths. They were the best way to relax and unwind after a stressful day. Ned was a peach going out to get him supplies. Which included his favorite beer. He took another drink and sighed.

It was nice getting away for a little bit. Ned's parents had told Steve to sleep when the baby does, but he also needed just to be alone and find himself again. It was hard getting used to being by himself again. He had his Little Bub with him 24/7 and now it was just him again. He cried. Steve tried to cover his mouth but he couldn't get himself to stop.

"Steve? Are you ok?"

The door opened with Ned bursting in. "What's wrong? Are you in pain?"

Steve could only shake his head. He couldn't stop crying. "I.. I'm... fine." He sobbed again.

Ned had the wide eyed look of someone in way over their head. Steve laughed, but it came out as a big sob. "I... miss... my... baby!" He knew he sounded crazy, but it was true, he missed having his constant companion. Little Bub was now Penny, their beautiful baby. He missed having her with him. He couldn't stop sobbing.

"Honey, you know she's here right?" Ned was rubbing his shoulders, but it wasn't making Steve feel any better.

"But... she's... not... in me.... anymore! I miss her!" He felt so stupid sobbing. What a lunatic. Their baby was perfect, nothing was wrong, everything was great and here he was sobbing in the tub.

"Oh Honey. I think I might know what this is." Ned leaned over and wrapped Steve in a hug. "This must be what new omega parents go through. Postpartum depression. It's such a shock to the body, giving birth and then your Little Bub that used to be with you isn't any longer. Right?"

Steve nodded his head. "Your baby is still here, but not inside you. And that's what's so sad right?"

Steve nodded his head again. "It's ok Honey. It's fine to be sad about that. They even have a name for it because it's so common."

Steve didn't feel stupid anymore. Just having Ned acknowledge the pain over not having his baby in him anymore helped to ease his pain. What an emotional rollercoaster. Pregnancy takes a toll on the body.

"I feel better now. I want to go to bed. I'm so tired." Ned helped him get out of the tub. He wrapped Steve in a big fluffy towel and walked him to their bedroom. Penny was sleeping in her crib, right next to Steve's side of the bed.

"See? She's right there. You can hold her and hug her anytime you want. She's the same Little Bub. Maybe I should get her a onesie with Little Bub printed on it. Would that help?"

Steve giggled. "It might." Ned pulled back the covers as Steve crawled into bed.

"Thank you for being so understanding. It came on me suddenly. I was fine one second and then sobbing the next." Ned crawled over to lie down next to Steve.

"Honey, I love you. And that's what postpartum depression is. Your hormones are out of whack as the pregnancy hormones are shut off. You will be in an emotional spin cycle for a while."

Steve didn't want to think of how long that would go on. This pregnancy thing was not a walk in the park.

"I'll sleep now. I'm tired."

"Good. You need sleep. You did all the heavy work. I think I'll take a nap too."

* * *

STEVE FELT BETTER about going to Henry and David's backyard than a public park. The backyard was more sheltered and there was no danger of rogue frisbees attacking them.

They were sitting on a quilt that Ned's mother gave them. It was a quilt that had been in their family. Steve didn't think they should put it on the ground, but should hang it on a wall. Ned's mother was insistent that it was just a practice quilt, and it was made for babies to be on. So, here it was on the grass in their friend's backyard.

Henry was sitting on the quilt with Elizabeth. She could crawl now. Her favorite destination was Penelope.

"She must think Penny is a big doll to play with."

Henry laughed. "I think you're right. She gets so mad when I pick her up and take her away from her new toy."

David and Ned were by the grill taking care of the steaks. Steve scooted and laid down on the quilt with Penny on his chest. He loved watching her eyes move around, trying to take it all in. Her thick black hair made her look like she was a few months old. It was so odd to think of babies growing hair when they weren't even born yet. He had never thought about it until he had his own baby.

"Aren't they a little miracle? I learned all of this in med school, none of it is new or a surprise. But experiencing it for myself is a different thing. It brings home what a miracle it is."

"It is a miracle. And they have such strong personalities right when they're so little. They're little butterballs of joy."

Henry lifted Elizabeth up and blew on her tummy. Her giggle was like heaven releasing joy into the world. Baby Penny even turned her head to look at the source of the noise.

"Hello everyone!" Penny walked over the wooden Japanese bridge to the backyard. "I can't wait to hold my little namesake!"

Steve smiled. He loved Penny's adoration of their baby, but he told Ned that he didn't like the look in her eye sometimes. He swore Penny would kidnap baby Penny one day and keep her.

Penny sat down on the edge of the quilt and held out her arms for Baby Penny. Steve lifted her off his chest and handed her over. Baby Penny would be spoiled rotten.

Steve was content to just lie down on the quilt and relax in the sun. It was nice to get outside. Ned was a great alpha. He knew what Steve needed.

Steve listened to the sounds of Elizabeth babbling, Penny cooing to Baby Penny, David and Ned talking by the grill. He smiled. Steve was the luckiest omega ever. He had the perfect family.

The End.

Thank you for reading! View Bella Bennet's catalog of books.

If you would like to know when I release a new book, and have a secret sale just for my newsletter subscribers, sign up for my newsletter. Yes, please, sign me up!